THE GRIFFIN AND THE ROSE

A Curoria Chronicles Novella

E.A. Almanza

Sarcastic Cat Writing, LLC

To Alex, my wonderful husband.

HARROW FIELD
PERCIPES PASS
MAULLERIES
CHAUVI
LAKE HOLIMEDA
DOVESPORT
AUBERVILLE
Westerlands, Thestitiunia

ONT TUNNELS
LEVILLE
AERIES LANDS
VICTORIE
MONSA
ADANES

Introduction

The Griffin and the Rose takes place primarily in between the year-long gap shown from Part One and Part Two in *The Guileful Rose*. This book is not necessary to be able to read and understand the main trilogy. However, if you want to know more about Theodmon and Amaria's relationship and how it developed within that year, this is a good book for that. It is recommended that *The Griffin and the Rose* be read after *The Guileful Rose,* but there is no set reading order.

As long as you've read Part One of *The Guileful Rose, The Griffin and the Rose* should be able to be understood and enjoyed. Additionally, in *The Griffin and the Rose* there are references to plot points, characters that are introduced, and locations that are shown later in the series.

The Griffin and the Rose is an adult fantasy novella made for those over the age of 18. Content readers may want to consider beforehand is gratuitous violence, gore, graphic consensual sexual content, references of drug usage, classism, misogyny (both external and internal), torture, death, and harsh language.

Table of Contents

The Griffin

Chapter One

The fields around Theodmon burned, the smoke choking him. Around him the mountains loomed closer, and as Theomdon looked at them, he realized that they weren't stone, but rather bodies.

"Archangel of Harréow Field," they hissed, sounding like serpents.

Theodmon's stomach lurched. These were all the Riams he had killed nearly a decade ago. He blinked, seeing the men's faces shift. No longer were they entirely faceless, with no distinguishable features. Now the faces were an eerily familiar one—each one resembled his father.

The blood drained from Theodmon, as if a spear impaled his heart.

"Theodmon," the corpses said.

"Stop," Theodmon begged, feeling as if he was flayed.

"Be as honorable as you're ruthless. Make me proud."

Theodmon's throat constricted as tears welled in his eyes. "Father."

The corpses stood up, blood pouring from their eyes, moving towards Theodmon. "The line must remain strong! Do not disappoint me!"

Theodmon woke up in a cold sweat, his blankets thrown off. He took a few shallow breaths, attempting to calm himself as his heart raced. It was just a dream.

Theodmon rolled over in bed, his skin sticking to the sheets. His feet hit the stone floor as he stood, moving toward the side table where he kept spare matches. He fumbled around in the dark until he struck the match, a small flame appearing; Theodmon placed the flame on the wick of the candle near his bed, illuminating the room around him.

The sweat on his back was cold as ice as he moved towards his curtains, opening them to reveal the stained glass griffin and forest etched into the window. He pushed the hidden door and stepped out onto the balcony.

Outside, the sun rose, the brilliant gold of the morning illuminating the reds and oranges of the changing trees. Theodmon breathed in, seeing his breath escape in a small puff into the October air. Down below, he saw the outline of houses in Chauvi, the city in the valley. Some days Theodmon couldn't believe he lived here, and even more importantly, that he was the lord over all of this.

He looked towards the forests and mountains, seeing birds flying overhead. This was not only his property, but it was his home. Stepping back inside his chambers, locking the door behind him, Theodmon swore that he would always protect his home.

And that meant preparing for threats. Yawning, Theodmon stretched before changing into a tunic, pants, and boots. He grabbed his sword as he headed towards the exit.

"I'm going to train," he told the guard outside his chambers. "I'll be back in two hours. Direct a maid to have a bath ready and to bring breakfast."

As he reached the training grounds, Theodmon set his sword against the wall and started his stretches. His breath was visible in the frigid air, and his tunic was too thin to do much to keep him warm. Shaking his arms and legs to warm up his muscles, Theodmon began jogging through the trails leading through the grounds of the estate and around Mount Mortensia.

He ran until his lungs burned, and when he passed the sword fighting grounds the first time, his friend, Lucas Bécharil, fell into step with him.

"You're late," Theodmon panted, sweat beading his forehead.

"Or you're early," Lucas countered. "How long have you been running?"

"One lap." Theodmon focused on his breathing.

"Let's do three."

Theodmon nodded, and the two of them continued their run, the only noises were the pounding of their feet and the chirping of birds.

Theodmon finished his three laps before Lucas, laying down in the dirt as Lucas did his last round. As his heartbeat slowed, Theodmon stood up and moved to the nearby well, pulling up a bucket of water to drink from. He was parched, slurping down the water as if he had never had a drink in his life. As he was doing so, Lucas returned, following the same ritual.

"Sword fighting or strength training?"

"Strength," Lucas muttered. "After I finish my last push-up I can just sleep on the ground."

Theodmon chuckled, laying himself down on the ground. "A hundred?"

"I hate you," Lucas said. "You're an asshole overachiever."

"You went to university just because you could," Theodmon pointed out with a snort. "I don't think you should call anyone an asshole overachiever."

Lucas cast him a dark look as he plopped himself on the ground. "What else are we doing?"

"Lemon squeezes and planks?"

"I'm going to kill you."

"Use it as inspiration for new torture techniques," Theodmon quipped, before beginning his push-ups. "You like that sort of thing, right?"

Lucas groaned, but still did the physical exercises as well.

Around his eightieth push-up, a page ran to Theodmon. "Apologies, my Lord," he said as Theodmon continued his push-ups. "We just received notice that Duke Raulet arrived in Chauvi."

Theodmon lowered himself to the ground, ending his set early. "You may go," he told the page. He looked over at Lucas. "Do you mind?"

"Is this to discuss your potential marriage?" Lucas smirked.

Theodmon chuckled, standing up from the ground.

"I think we should showcase your push-ups for Duke Raulet. Nothing says husbandry like-"

"Next time we train," Theodmon interrupted, "I'm whacking you with a sword until you bruise."

Lucas snorted. "You say that like you're better than me."

"Will you tell the kitchens to prepare a feast for Duke Raulet's arrival?" Theodmon asked. "I expect you and your wife to be there tonight."

Lucas rolled his eyes. "Go."

Theodmon pulled himself out of the large stone basin, clean and his muscles relaxed from the hot water. He wouldn't mind sharing this with a wife. That was why Aaron Raulet was here–to discuss marrying his daughter to Theodmon.

And Theodmon wanted to marry Aaron Raulet's daughter. The family was absurdly wealthy, and with all the threats the Westerlands defended against, being the closest Thestitiunian duchy to both Rindria and Morroek, his army needed the funds.

To Amaria Raulet's misfortune, but perhaps to Theodmon's benefit, her last engagement ended dramatically. Aaron, for some reason, told Amaria's last fiancé, an Avonnian duke named Lyseno Vypren, that he was no longer to marry her mere months before their planned wedding. Lyseno Vypren, in a rage, attacked Amaria, attempting to cut her open in front of Aaron.

The girl survived. Two months later Aaron announced that he was looking for another candidate. And Theodmon's sources indicated that Aaron was interested in keeping Amaria closer to home now.

Theodmon pulled on his clothing, ensuring he looked his best to make a good impression with Duke Raulet. He stepped out of the washing room to his chambers, seeing maids setting down his breakfast. "Are my sister and brother awake?"

"Lady Celestine had breakfast summoned to her sitting rooms," the maid answered.

"And Lord Aloysius?"

The maid looked at her feet, her face turning red.

Theodmon sighed. "You may go."

The maids scurried out and he slumped in his chair as he took a big bite of his eggs. Gods, he hoped Aloysius was just sleeping in after a long exhausting day and not sleeping off one variety of debauchery or another.

Chapter Two

Theodmon wrinkled his nose in disgust as he came into his brother's rooms, smelling the stench of alcohol and sex. On the bed were three naked women, Aloysius sleeping in the middle of them.

His nostrils flared. Aaron Raulet, a man they needed to impress and who was notoriously pious and uptight about whores, was arriving at the castle today. And Aloysius knew this and he chose to invite brothel girls into Forteresse les Blanche.

He roughly shook one of the girls awake.

"Get out," he told her, her eyes widening in fear. "Wake up the others and leave."

Her lip quivered.

"Have you been paid?" He asked as the girl woke the other workers.

"Not yet, my Lord." She pulled on her flimsy dress which somehow showed just as much as when she was naked.

"Have your brothel send the estate a bill," Theodmon commanded, wishing he had money on him. "Discreetly. Ask for Lord Henri Delaluna, if you need to speak to anybody."

The woman paled, the other two awake and dressed behind her. Theodmon held back a sigh at the woman's small-minded fear at hearing the mind-reader's name. "Lord Delaluna won't hurt you. Leave."

The women scurried out like frightened mice. He watched them leave, and then directed his attention to his unconscious brother, empty alcohol bottles and a brilliant turquoise powder surrounding him.

Verta. Theodmon cursed. The damned drug was a powerful hallucinogen. Of course his idiot brother was high on it. "Guards!"

The guards ran in.

"Get me a bucket of ice water."

Of course Aloysius would do this today. His brother had no sense of responsibility. When their father died Theodmon had to run the Westerlands, follow through with Ophelia's marriage alliance, and manage the army. Aloysius got to whore, drink, and get high. And for what? Aloysius hadn't even been there when Father died.

A guard came with a metal bucket, water lapping over the sides. Theodmon nodded curtly, dismissing him. As the guard left, Theodmon paced around the bed, surveying how Aloysius was laying. Once the door shut behind the guard, Theodmon threw the bucket of water onto his brother.

"What the hell?" Aloysius fell out of bed, screaming.

"Get up." Theodmon looked towards the empty liquor bottles and the drug paraphernalia. "We've an important visitor today."

"Are you seriously considering marrying her?" Aloysius pulled a towel from his drawers. "That alliance with Tressidil from a marriage to Mylisana Caeltra may be more beneficial; Raulets are Thestitiunian. They'll align with us on most things by that alone."

"She's rich."

"And a Raulet. You can't trust them," Aloysius countered. "And she comes with that shit with Lyseno Vypren. I don't understand why your strategic brain isn't running away from this match."

"How the fuck are you coherent?" Theodmon snapped.

"I've built a tolerance." Aloysius smirked. "You should try it sometimes."

"No."

"It'd make you less of an ass."

Theodmon sighed, sinking on the bed. "She's not a bad match. A Raulet is a Raulet. I'm not saying I'll marry her on that alone, but I'll hear what Aaron proposes." He looked over at Aloysius. "Bathe."

"You're trying to impress her father." Aloysius snorted. "You really want to marry her."

"And what if I do? She has a large dowry. And I can likely leverage more from her father because of the incident with Vypren. According to all my sources, he wasn't successful in carving out her womb, so she can still provide heirs. Vypren and I don't have an alliance and I've strong alliances with other Avonnian states. What's the negative in marrying her?"

"She's Thestitiunian," Aloysius said. "Unless there's some rare inner conflict going on within the empire, foreign alliances are more important."

"The Caeltra's aren't as rich. Troops need money. Celestine needs money for her marriage."

"Celestine doesn't want to be married. She's seen Ophelia married off to a man as old as father, and the poor girl is twenty two with four kids and another one on the way."

"Then money for her maintenance at a temple," Theodmon amended.

"Are you sure you're not blinded by Amaria Raulet's beauty? I've not heard much about Mylisana Caeltra's looks, but we've both seen Amaria at Imperial Court Events-"

"I'd like to be attracted to my wife," Theodmon clipped. "I'm not a degenerate like you. Did you need to have three whores?"

"Despite how much you pretend otherwise, we are rich," Aloysius slurred.

Theodmon turned his back to Aloysius. "Three whores is excessive, regardless of financial ability. What happened to tiring one out?"

"You're the one looking to get married." Aloysius stretched his arms upwards. "And don't be a hypocrite. We both know you did that yourself a time or two.

Is wanting to court Amaria the reason why you dismissed Livia? Can't have her father seeing your mistre–"

Theodmon pinned Aloysius to the bedpost, looking at his red rimmed eyes. "How much verta did you snort?"

"Does it matter? Your guest should be thrilled, I'm giving his duchy money–"

"You're unbelievable. Would it kill you to not be a fuck-up for one day?"

As soon as he said it, Theodmon felt a twinge of regret. That regret quickly dissipated as Aloysius vomited, and Theodmon was splattered with brown chunks.

Theodmon unpinned Aloysius, pushing him away from him. "Stay out of sight." He pulled Aloysius's blanket from the bed, scrubbing the chunks off himself.

He would have Katerina, the resident healing mage, come and put Aloysius to sleep and confine him to his chambers while Aaron Raulet was here. And he'd get himself a bath. Immediately.

"You can't hide me forever. If you marry this Raulet girl, her father will eventually see me."

"By that time she'd be my wife." Aaron could do his worst but once Theodmon married and, better yet, impregnated Amaria, the worst Aaron could do was severely limited.

"Aren't you concerned about Amaria?" Aloysius asked. "Rumors say she's *non-traditional* in some respects."

Theodmon gave a small snort. "Are those non-traditional qualities anything to do with her abilities as a wife and mother?"

"She tortures people," Aloysius said. "And she's apparently really good at it."

Theodmon shrugged. "An added advantage. She can truly manage all of my affairs while I'm at war."

Aloysius's eyes narrowed. "You actually don't care? I would have thought you would have wanted a perfect feminine flower."

"All Raulets are roses. Besides, Amaria is feminine from all reports-we've both seen her."

"Yes, she's adept at court politics and beautiful," Aloysius said sharply. "But she tortures people. She helps run *her father's* affairs. Aren't you concerned that we're welcoming a beautiful snake into our family?"

"If she's untrustworthy, at least we got her money," Theodmon shrugged. "But as you said, we're both Thestitiunian. There's a chance we can work together and that beautiful snake will be an asset to our family. Besides, where was this mentality when you were fucking Haerdnor Raulet?"

"It was a summer fling," Aloysius grumbled. "Not marriage. And besides, Haerdnor is the least dangerous one in that family."

Theodmon raised an eyebrow, making a scoffing noise. "I'll send maids to help clean up here and prepare a bath. Katerina will be in to help...." Theodmon's nose crinkled as he looked Aloysius up and down. "Try not to ruin this for me."

"If you wanna fuck a Raulet, you can go for a cousin." Aloysius said as Theodmon walked towards the exit.

Pausing, Theodmon chuckled darkly. "No."

Aloysius rolled his eyes. "Why not? Why do you want *this* Raulet?"

As much as Theodmon hated to admit it, Aloysius had a point. Why was he so fixated on Amaria Raulet? He had never interacted with her, except in passing when both of them had to be at the Imperial Court or other formal events. She was captivating in a way he couldn't explain; and although the end of her engagement was horrific, Theodmon was glad it happened.

"Because she's the best one. I want a Raulet from the main line, not a cousin."

Behind him, Aloysius shook his head. "Be careful your ambition doesn't get us killed."

Chapter Three

"**D**uke Raulet," Theodmon greeted as he stepped into his office. Aaron Raulet was sitting on the large red sofa and the duke moved for his cane as Theodmon entered, trying to stand.

"Please, there's no need," Theodmon said, holding up a hand in protest. "We're both ruling leaders of Thestitiunian duchies and if all goes well you will soon be my father-in-law."

Aaron chuckled. "How considerate," he said, the words as slippery as algae floating on a pond. "Why do you want to marry my daughter?"

"I need a wife." Theodmon sat down on the sofa across from Aaron. "I've been ruling for nearly a decade and with the constant wars, the need for heirs-"

"That's why you want to marry in general," Aaron interrupted. "Why do you want to marry *my* daughter?"

Theodmon sat back, looking at the chessboard on the coffee table in front of him. "Do you play?"

Aaron looked at Theodmon critically. "Yes."

"Do you mind if I'm white?"

Aaron chuckled, his eyes flashing as he continued looking over Theodmon. "I prefer black anyways."

"Convenient." Theodmon's hand hovered over a pawn as he moved it. "And I want to marry your daughter for a multitude of reasons."

"Her dowry?" Aaron moved his own piece.

"I'm not going to pretend it's not a substantial interest." Theodmon moved a knight. "Let's be honest with each other-it'll make these negotiations smoother."

Aaron moved a knight to mirror Theodmon's piece. "I've not agreed to let you propose to her."

"If you were to, and I think it would be beneficial for your daughter if you did." Theodmon moved another pawn. "I'm interested in marrying your daughter because she intrigues me."

"So you're a collector?" Aaron moved a black pawn.

Theodmon surveyed the board. "I've always been partial to the idea of having a love match, or at the very least a decent relationship in my marriage. It's the one piece of idealism I've been able to maintain." He picked up his knight again, moving it to a place where he knew it would be taken. "I think there might be a chance of that with Amaria."

Aaron chuckled, his rook taking Theodmon's knight. "Have you ever interacted with her?"

"Only in passing," Theodmon moved his pawn to take Aaron's rook. "But I hear she has a particularly interesting skill set. She's more talented than most men in the dungeons, apparently, and I'd have no objection if she continued that skill at Forteresse les Blanche."

Aaron moved a pawn, his eyes unbreaking from Theodmon.

"She'd be free to continue helping you with your affairs. I won't stifle her."

"While she's pregnant with heirs?" Aaron asked.

"From what I've heard, Amaria is capable of making her own judgments." Theodmon moved his chess piece. "Providing heirs is a priority, but that would be the case regardless of who she married. How many men would offer this arrangement?"

"Perhaps I don't want my daughter in a dungeon any more."

"Your Grace, you could do me the courtesy of not lying to my face in my own home. If you didn't want her in a dungeon, you wouldn't still have her torturing prisoners. I heard she did quite a few last month." He met Aaron's eyes. "You're a practical man. Why waste her talents?"

Aaron gave a soft smile, moving a chess piece. "I want assurances."

"Assurances?"

"That you won't harm my daughter."

Theodmon crossed his arms. "I've never hit a woman, if that's what you're implying."

"I've heard of your reputation," Aaron said. "Gallant. Honorable. I can't help but question how much of it is true, because you are also a ruthless military commander. Honor and ruthlessness are antithetical to each other."

"I'm not going to beat my wife."

"If you do, I'll bring this entire mountain down on you," Aaron said. "I'm an earth mage."

"So is she," Theodmon said. "More powerful than you."

Aaron gave a barking laugh. "I suppose she is."

Theodmon's eyes narrowed. He watched as Aaron shifted in his seat. "Is she healing well after-"

"Why do you ask?" Aaron leaned towards Theodmon as his lips curled downward.

"Because we have to plan a wedding and I'm not interested in consummating the marriage if she's bleeding through stitches."

"We haven't agreed."

"We're close." Theodmon moved his rook in position to take Aaron's king. "You wouldn't bring a mountain down on me for hitting my wife unless that wife was your daughter."

Aaron moved his king out of danger. "You're clever. I'll give you that, Marquis."

"And what do you get from this hypothetical agreement?" Theodmon ignored the compliment.

"Your army when needed."

"We're Thestitiunian. If you were attacked you'd have my army."

"Who said anything about defending attacks? I want to cripple Morroek and Rindria. I need a stronger offensive. You have one of the strongest military forces in Thestitiunia." Aaron inclined his head with a smirk. "Besides, I want to keep my daughter close. You're perfect in both regards."

"I won't lead my men to a slaughter," Theodmon said. "But we will offer aid as long as I have a say in any invasion."

Aaron gave a smile that didn't quite reach his eyes. "Naturally."

Theodmon's jaw locked. Perhaps he would regret marrying this girl, but he needed the money for his troops. "So do we have an agreement?"

Aaron sighed. "I suppose we should discuss her dowry."

Theodmon moved his queen at a diagonal across the board, taking Aaron's king. "I've heard it's substantial."

"Two hundred horses. Twenty pounds of pearls, sapphires, and diamonds. Fifty thousand gold dragons."

Theodmon forced himself to keep his face neutral, as to not show his surprise at the sheer volume of Amaria's wealth. He knew it was large, but having it laid out was something else entirely.

"Seventy-five thousand gold dragons, twenty-five of it goes to pay for my army's debts," Theodmon countered, starting off the negotiations with something he expected Aaron to immediately dismiss.

"Sixty," Aaron countered.

"Sixty-five thousand dragons and enough bushels of grain to feed the army for a year." Theodmon barely believed his luck. He was marrying Amaria Raulet and he may be receiving an even larger dowry than he ever anticipated.

"Fifty-eight thousand and the bushels of grain."

Theodmon grinned, holding out his hand for Aaron to shake. "Deal. Shall I get someone to draw up the engagement contract?"

Aaron nodded as he stood up, groaning as he gripped his cane. "When do you wish to marry her?"

"How soon are you willing to part with her?"

"By mid-summer," Aaron said.

Theodmon watched Aaron grip his cane as he hobbled out of the room. "Your Grace, may I have permission to write to your daughter, proposing to her through letter?" It was a formality, a nicety, that had no bearing on anything in the engagement or future marriage. Amaria was engaged to him once Aaron and he signed those documents.

"She'd like that." Aaron's voice was impossibly soft. "Thank you, Marquis Chauvignon."

Chapter Four

Theodmon stepped into the parlor where Lucas and Henri were playing cards, grinning. "You can't tell anyone yet."

Lucas dropped his hand of cards. "You're marrying her, aren't you?"

Theodmon nodded. "We're not announcing it. Not until I can write to her once."

"When's the wedding?" Henri asked.

"Mid-summer," Theodmon said as he determined that he would find Aloysius in his rooms later to tell him the news, if only to rub it in his face.

"So the timeline is what?" Henri watched Theodmon with concern. "You write to her with the nicety of pretending to ask for her hand, get her response, then announce your marriage to the court? The wedding invites would have to go out soon after."

"It's not a nicety," Theodmon protested, wanting to keep up the illusion of the lie. "No woman wants to be passed around as if she's property. She at least wants to have a say."

"But she doesn't," Henri said. "Amaria can't refuse."

"You know her don't you?" Theodmon focused on Henri. "You're both Extractors."

"Thanks for noticing," Henri said dryly. "And yes, I've worked with her."

"Tell me about her."

"You didn't know anything about your future wife when you negotiated the engagement?" Lucas snickered.

"I know she's wealthy, beautiful, a powerful mage, and has some degree of intelligence and ruthlessness." Theodmon cast Lucas a dark look. "Most grooms only know that much about their future wives, I'm asking Henri what he knows as her associate."

"I'd consider her my friend, actually," Henri said.

"Then talk to me," Theodmon said. "Her last fiancé was awful. We all know Lyseno Vypren is a putrid fool. I want to know how to make her life here comforting." He remembered how terrified Ophelia had been when he walked her down the aisle at her wedding, and his sister hadn't been mutilated by a potential husband.

Henri looked at Theodmon, no doubt reading his mind. "She's proud of her family—you could have roses in your rooms, have some blue fabric for dresses."

"What about a blanket with her House colors and roses hidden under the comforters in our bed?" Theodmon said, thinking out loud.

"That's touching," Henri said.

"Who would have thought you were that sensitive," Lucas muttered under his breath.

Theodmon ignored him. "What else?"

Henri blinked. "Uh, she's a powerful mage."

"Stuff I don't know."

"She's afraid of the dark. Most fire mages are," he added hastily. "It's not a hidden fact."

Theodmon looked over at Lucas, wondering if Henri was so tight-lipped because he didn't want to betray Amaria's confidence, or worse the privacy of her own mind. "Lucas, would you mind leaving so Henri and I can talk privately?"

Lucas shrugged, standing up to leave. "I suppose I'll have to go see my own wife," he said dryly. "Theo, why don't you just ask Amaria about herself when you meet her?"

"I will. But I still want to make it a little less scary for her."

Lucas snorted. "For a pragmatic you're disgustingly romantic."

Once the door shut behind Lucas, Theodmon leaned forward on his knees, his eyes unblinking from Henri's. "I appreciate you wanting to respect her privacy. But please tell me what I can do to make her comfortable. I've heard enough about Vypren...." He trailed off taking a deep breath, composing his thoughts.

"I think the blanket is a good idea," Henri said. "She likes apples, lemons, and pomegranates. She's very organized and efficient. By tradition, you could have embroidery tools ready so she could start the union tapestry as soon as possible, I believe she'd appreciate that."

"What other foods does she like?"

"Seafood."

"Something we can get for the wedding," Theodmon amended. "Seafood of that amount may be difficult this far inland."

Henri chuckled. "Boar."

Theodmon nodded, determining he would hunt down a boar himself for the wedding. "Tell me more."

Henri laughed. "Speak to her. Lucas was right, but I think what you're doing will help."

"Would she like gifts during the wedding tour?"

Henri looked at Theodmon pensively. "I never expected you to be one caught up in romance."

"Me either," Theodmon admitted. "I'm being stupid, aren't I? I don't even know this girl. She may despise me-"

"She thought you were attractive." Henri's face flushed as he averted his eyes from Theodmon. "At jousts. Along with most other ladies. Before you ask, no, I'm not repeating the details."

"So, she won't despise me because she thinks I'm attractive?" Theodmon snorted. "Helpful."

"And because you obviously care about her feelings," Henri added. "These small things in her first week here, they'll add up. I have to ask though, why all the effort?"

"She's to be my wife."

"But you don't have to do this for a wife. Would you do this for any other woman?"

No. The admission hit Theodmon like he had been kicked by a horse. "Amaria Raulet has always been...dynamic. She fascinates me." He cleared his throat. "Besides, she is infinitely more wealthy and powerful than most–an alliance between our families will be more productive if Lady Raulet and I like each other."

"Lady Raulet," Henri snorted.

"Shut up," Theodmon said, departing from Henri to head to his offices. He had to write a letter to Amaria.

It was January.

The invites for the July wedding were written and sealed, ready to be sent out with a rider as soon as the snow stopped falling. Amaria had never written him back, but Aaron confirmed the details. Now, it was time for Theodmon to announce his engagement to his court.

His fingers drummed on the table as he waited for the soup to be delivered by the servants.

Next to him, Aloysius was on his third glass of mead.

"Can you not?" Theodmon hissed.

"It's a celebration, isn't it?" Aloysius's words slurred. "You marrying Amaria Raulet? You did it–you made your dreams come true."

"It's not been announced yet. Have some self-control."

Aloysius rolled his eyes. "You're not my father."

Theodmon felt as if he had been punched in the gut. He ground his teeth together. "I'm still the head of this household."

Would his father be happy for him? Had Theodmon done a good job in maintaining their family? Would his father be proud of them? Theodmon felt tears pricking in the corner of his eyes. He swallowed the lump in his throat, deciding he needed to start drinking soon to avoid these thoughts.

He stood up, nodding to the heralder who blew his horn, gaining everyone's attention. Theodmon took the glass of mead from Aloysius. "I've an announcement. I'll be getting married soon, in July."

The hall burst into scattered whispers.

"My bride is Lady Amaria Raulet." Theodmon raised the glass of mead. "To my engagement. Enjoy the feast." He took a drink, sitting down as conversation rang across the great hall.

"Now you can drink." He gave Aloysius the glass back. "And you backwash."

Aloysius downed the rest of the goblet. "Get your own drink next time."

Chapter Five

She was beautiful. Theodmon couldn't think of anything else as he stood at the podium, watching Aaron escort Amaria down the aisle. Even though her face was covered by the heavy veil, Theodmon could tell she was gorgeous, dressed to stun others with her beauty.

Her wedding dress was loaded with pearls, rubies, and sapphires, an ostentatious but not unwarranted display of wealth. He looked over at Aloysius, who stood next to him as his best man. Aloysius shrugged, a slight smirk appearing.

Theodmon tore his eyes away from his brother and back to his bride. She had reached the altar. Amaria kissed her father on the cheek, and Aaron handed her off to Theodmon. "Remember," Aarron whispered. "You live on a mountain."

How could I forget? Theodmon gave Aaron a curt nod, before taking Amaria's hands in his, giving Amaria what he hoped was a comforting smile as the priest gave the traditional speeches and blessings. Then, it was time to exchange the rings.

Theodmon slipped the tear-drop-shaped ruby onto Amaria's ring finger. Amaria took Theodmon's hand as she placed a simple gold band, a streak of rubies running through it, on his hand.

"Marquis, you may lift the bride's veil, show her off as your wife, and then kiss your new Marchioness for the gods and men to see," the priest said. Theodmon smiled at Amaria, his hands reaching for her veil, throwing it over her head.

Theodmon's breath caught in his chest as she gave him a small, close-lipped smile in return. Small, cascading waves framed her face. Her face flushed as he continued to stare at her.

Despite that, with her slightly raised brow, it seemed almost as if she was inviting him to challenge her. And her silver eyes sparkled as he gently placed his hands on her waist, turning her towards the crowd.

She was warm, radiant, beautiful and utterly captivating. And she was his.

"We bless this union," the priest called behind them.

Theodmon noticed that Amaria seemed stiff as he turned her to face him. Their lips connected, and the crowd applauded. They pulled away, and briefly smiled at each other.

"I now pronounce these two lawfully wed!" the priest announced. "Please remain seated as Marquis and Marchioness Chauvignon leave the hall."

Theodmon and Amaria left the hall in a blur, heading down to the temple to pray to the gods privately as husband and wife. Other provinces had a more practical tradition of going to the temple after the consummation and after the guests left. Westannis, however, preferred to be difficult in their traditions.

Theodmon and Amaria were back in the great hall, sitting at the head of the table, greeting guests.

"Tell me about yourself," Theodmon directed when there was a lull.

Amaria looked at him wide eyed, momentarily a startled animal being hunted. "My favorite color is turquoise," she said, her tone neutral.

"More blue or green?" Theodmon asked.

"What?" Amaria blinked up at him.

"The turquoise you like, is it more blue or green?" Theodmon clarified. This was like pulling teeth, both of them were awkward with each other. What a great start to a marriage.

It's an arranged marriage, Theodmon reminded himself. *They all start off awkward.*

Amaria tilted her head. "Blue. Like the sea by Raulle."

She looked at him expectantly, and perhaps, Theodmon realized with a jolt, she wanted him to share something about himself as well. Theodmon chuckled, more at himself than anything else. "Mine is orange. Not a bright orange, but more muted. Think of the leaves in fall."

"I bet fall is beautiful here."

"I hope you enjoy it," Theodmon told her sincerely, internally cursing as a guest approached their table. "If you want, I'll bring you to festivals."

He wished he could have told her more about the festivals with the candied apples, roasted turkey legs, dancing, archery, and horseback riding. Sometimes, there were even acrobats doing acts of daring, contorting their bodies in impossible ways at impossible heights.

Unfortunately, Theodmon didn't get the chance. He had to greet guests. All of them were pompous pricks with inflated ideas of their importance. Theodmon would have preferred a smaller wedding with only friends and family–not every noble living on the continent.

As if Lucas were somehow summoned, he approached Theodmon, giving him the quick, formal bow. Theodmon stood up, bear clapping Lucas in a hug, interrupting the bow. "Lucas!"

Lucas chuckled, pulling away.

"This is Lord Lucas Bécharil," Theodmon introduced Lucas to Amaria. "Lucas, this is my wife, Marchioness Amaria Chauvignon."

It felt strange to call her that. And yet, it fit perfectly.

"Pleasure, my Lord," Amaria inclined her head towards Lucas. Amaria addressed Juliette, Lucas's wife, "My Lady." Theodmon's brows bunched together until he remembered that Juliette greeted Amaria when she first arrived at Forteresse les Blanche.

"Would you like to dance with me later?" Amaria asked the other woman.

Juliette beamed. "I'd love that, thank you, my Lady."

Juliette and Lucas moved out of the way, headed towards a table near the front. Behind them, Aloysius, bowed, pausing to move around the table to sit next to Theodmon.

"The formalities are stiff," Aloysius complained.

"We still have to do them," Theodmon chastised, pretending to drink from his goblet to hide his moving lips. He agreed with Aloysius though, but insulting a bunch of nobles and jeopardizing political, financial, and military relationships weren't something he was anxious to do.

Amaria was speaking with Theodmon's sisters, and when Theodmon looked over, they were gone, a lull in the never ending guests.

"I'd love to go to those festivals with you, my Lord Husband," Amaria whispered to Theodmon, a smile frozen on her face.

"Theodmon," he corrected. The identifier "my Lord Husband" felt excessive. "I don't want us to be overly formal."

Amaria placed her hand over his, squeezing it. "I agree."

Theodmon smiled at her, feeling as if the sun were breaking through storm clouds. There was hope this relationship wouldn't be strained forever.

And then more guests came. By the time Theodmon had to greet Durek Svilas from Morroek he was ready to go to bed and not emerge from his chambers for days.

"Pleasure to see you again, Duke Svilas." Amaria's voice was sweet as honey.

"I share the same sentiment," Svilas said. "It's the same delight I have when you visit in Morroek."

Theodmon took a sip of his drink, hiding the curling of his mouth. He had almost forgotten Amaria conducted her father's affairs–trading and diplomacy–in Morroek. Theodmon supposed he let Amaria do that so he could infuriate the Morrians who had a rather restrictive view of women in society.

"Enjoy the meal," Amaria said, dismissing Svilas.

Svilas's face hardened, but he bowed. "Thank you, Marquis and Marchioness Chauvignon."

Behind him, Henri came forward, a hand running through his hair. Theodmon stood up, pulling him into a hug similar to the one he gave Lucas.

Henri chuckled. "He despises you."

"It doesn't take a mind reader to know that," Theodmon said.

"Congratulations." Henri turned towards Amaria. "I'm glad we aren't losing you from our order."

"You know the emperor would never allow that," Amaria said.

The two mages looked at each other, and Theodmon felt like an invasive outsider for a moment. The two seemed to be in some sort of mental conversation, an intense argument only the two of them would ever know about.

And then Henri bowed. "Congratulations to you both."

As he departed, Theodmon looked at Amaria with raised brows.

Tears welled in her eyes. "I suspect some of our guests killed my friend."

Theodmon internally cursed. He'd heard about the attack on Provincia Palencia.

"I heard about that." Theodmon's hand moved to hold hers. "I know it won't bring her back, but I'm sorry for your loss."

Amaria sniffed. "Thank you. Please, not now."

Theodmon nodded, squeezing her hand. He understood not wanting to cry in front of everyone, and the notion that some conversations would breach a dam. "It looks as if we have Avonnian guests approaching," he said, hoping to distract her. "Hopefully there'll be food soon."

As he talked with the Avonnians, Theodmon noticed that Amaria was stiffly sitting next to him, a flash of anger momentarily appearing in her eyes before she stared blankly ahead of her. Theodmon recognized that expression because after his father died he had often had the same one. She was carefully composing herself, but despite her best efforts, the slightest inconvenience would cause her façade to crumble.

Theodmon didn't want her to break down at their wedding. Today was a happy day-he didn't want an international scandal to ruin it. Amaria was exhausted and she couldn't continue greeting guests.

Theodmon stood up, holding his hand out to her. "Would you like to dance?"

She took his hand, giving off a heavy sigh. "Absolutely."

Around them, as Theodmon danced with Amaria, the musicians' violins wove in beautiful notes and harmonies. They were married and all that remained was the consummation. Theodmon tightened his grip around Amaria's waist. He hated the idea of consummation-he had already banned spectators, that tradition was one that needed to burn.

But even taking care of that element, it still felt nerve wracking-he wanted his new wife to be comfortable here, but he wasn't stupid enough to believe tonight wouldn't be terrifying for her. He looked into her silver eyes as they waltzed and hoped that one day they wouldn't be as stiff with each other as they were right now.

After all, smaller miracles had happened.

The Rose

Chapter Six

The morning after her wedding, Amaria sat crossed legged in the large four poster bed, pulling spools of embroidery floss from a basket. Amaria liked embroidery. She enjoyed stabbing something and making something beautiful from it.

Her fingers brushed over the large canvas, picking up a small charcoal pencil. She'd frame the design with roses and swords, as if the tapestry were a painting and her border was the frame. Biting her lip, Amaria drew in the design, the charcoal smudging over her hands. She'd use golden thread for the swords, red and green for the roses. The only noise was the scratching of the pencil over the woven canvas.

Finally, she finished the outline of her design and sighed as she placed the cloth on the bed, going to wash the black from her hands at the small basin placed in the washroom attached to her chambers. She breathed in, surveying her new home. These chambers were large, but still cozy, although the amount of red made Amaria's head spin. Red was such an aggressive color for a bedroom. She preferred the blue she grew up with.

She dunked her hands in the basin, the cold water sending a jolt through her. Clenching her jaw she pulled out her hands, forcing her magic to weave out, incrementally warming the water. Once that was done, Amaria dunked her hands again, picking up the lemon soap laying nearby and scrubbing.

Theodmon had said he liked lemon soap their first night here, in the bath. She rubbed her hands together, the black charcoal washing off. Would he like other lemon things? Amaria should have brought lemons with her from Raulle.

How would I have known that? Amaria chided herself as she dried her hands, stepping back into the main chambers.

She hadn't seen Theodmon since this morning, when they were woken by the servants to get their sheets as proof the marriage had been consummated. She threaded a needle, biting her lip. He had been so kind and gentle last night. It hurt when he fled in the morning towards the training grounds.

Perhaps he regretted marrying her. *Stop it.* She told herself. *It's done.*

For the next few hours, Amaria worked on the border, finishing half of one side of the tapestry by the time the sun had set and the candles had to be lit. She was doing a woven wheel stitch for the center of her roses when Theodmon entered the room.

"Have you been here all day?"

Amaria nodded, tying her stitch.

"You didn't have to stay here," Theodmon said.

"I figured you had business you were busy with." Amaria looked up at Theodmon. "And I wanted to make some progress on the Union Tapestry."

"It could wait until after we come back from our wedding tour." Theodmon took her hands in his as he kneeled beside her. "I'd hoped I could show you around Forteresse les Blanche before we left."

"I was hoping to get the border done before we left—it's the only thing I know what to do with the tapestry right now." She squeezed his hand, smiling at him. "But, thank you. Could you show me around tomorrow, when it's light?"

Theodmon stood up, moving to sit on the bed next to her. "I'd enjoy that. Are you ready to come to dinner with me?"

Amaria blinked, realizing she hadn't eaten all day.

"It's a small affair with Aloysius, Celestine, my mother, Lord Delaluna, Lord and Lady Bécharil. And I've invited your Lady, ah, Nicoletta Lemaire, and her fiancé, Earl Astasuel."

"Are my siblings and father not invited?"

Theodmon ran his hand through his hair. "They can be, if you wish. I was trying to show you how dinners here would be. Ease you into it. My mother is difficult."

"So is my father," Amaria said. "Perhaps each of their difficulties will cancel the other one out."

Theodmon laughed. "I'll extend the invitation to Haerdnor, Catalina, and Aaron." He turned towards a nearby guard, barking orders for him to find Amaria's family with an invite.

Amaria smiled, forcing down the lump in her throat. "That sounds nice." Theodmon was making an enormous effort in ensuring she was welcomed and comfortable here. "I appreciated the Raulet blanket under the comforter," she told him. "It's just all so different here."

Theodmon laughed. "Wait until our tour. You'll see more of the Westerlands."

"Mountains and forests," Amaria remarked.

"It's different from islands and farmland," Theodmon agreed. "But it's home."

It wasn't Amaria's home yet. She still felt like an outsider–a stranger who hadn't fully been welcomed. But she hoped one day she wouldn't feel that way. She looked down at her dress, the cotton plain without any stitching or intricate layers. "How casual is this dinner?" Amaria ran her hands over a fold in her dress. This dress was fine for remaining in her chambers all day, but for a dinner so soon after the wedding...

"There's some stragglers from the wedding," Theodmon said. "If you're worried about appearances-"

"Thank you." Amaria interrupted without a thought. Her face turned red as she realized her mistake and she flinched away from Theodmon, expecting a slap. "I apologize, I didn't mean to interrupt."

Theodmon's jaw locked. "Vypren beat you during your engagement to him, didn't he?"

The limited times she'd seen Vypren during their engagement, he'd found ways to corner her, to isolate her, and to hurt her. "No," Amaria lied on instinct. She forced her eyes shut, biting her lip. She didn't want to lie to Theodmon. Why was she lying to him? "Yes," she whispered.

"I'm not going to hurt you," Theodmon said kindly. "We're having a conversation. I want you to respond to me."

"But I didn't let you finish speaking." Amaria hated how fragile and weak she was. She vowed to kill Vypren someday. She shouldn't be so terrified of him, of other men, because of him.

Theodmon snorted. "I'm not that insecure." He cast a glance around the room, his gaze pausing on the still unpacked trunks. "Have the maids not finished unpacking?"

Amaria shook her head.

"And I guess they've not packed for our wedding tour. We leave next week—I'll have them finish up while we're at dinner. Do you need a maid to help you change?"

"How formal is this dinner?"

"It's small," Theodmon said. "So not overly formal. Do you need a maid to help you change?"

Amaria shook her head once more. If this dinner wasn't overly formal, she could dress herself. Already she knew that she would pick out a decorative overdress and a few pieces of jewelry to bring the outfit up to par. "Please give me a moment." She strode towards the chest, rummaging inside until she pulled out a golden and white garment.

She pulled it over herself, stepping in front of the mirror to adjust the strings. Underneath the dress, you could still see the blue of her dress poking through.

Amaria smiled, enjoying how she looked, before she moved towards her vanity, threading in sapphire and diamond earrings.

"Let me." Theodmon placed the matching necklace around her neck.

Amaria smiled at him through her reflection in the mirror. Theodmon fumbled with the clasp for a few moments, but he soon secured the jewels around her neck.

Theodmon stepped away, allowing her to stand. "Are you ready?"

Amaria nodded, looping her arm through his outstretched arm. "I suppose we might get an early tour of your home."

"Our home," Theodmon corrected. Amaria nodded in agreement, although the notion of Forteresse les Blanche being her home was still an alien concept.

They departed from their rooms, Theodmon pointing out suits of armor and paintings not only as landmarks, but to explain his family's history and genealogy. Amaria listened, giving Theodmon a soft smile.

Theodmon walked past two doors and the guards opened them, revealing a bridge, tall branches of evergreens scratching against the stone as the summer air floated past them.

"Are we taking the long way around?" Amaria asked as Theodmon guided her down the bridge. "Won't we be late?" Amaria cast a furtive glance behind her. "I don't think I should be out after dark–"

Theodmon's face contorted. "I forgot. You're afraid of the dark."

She had told him her first night here, needing candles lit throughout the night. Amaria nodded, fear bubbling in her stomach. She outstretched her hands, summoning fire to lick her fingertips, and only her fingertips. The last thing she needed was to appear at dinner with burnt clothes.

"We can go back inside." Theodmon stepped closer to her in a protective stance. He guided her back towards the door, banging on it with a command to the guards inside to let him back in.

Amaria and Theodmon stepped back inside Forteresse les Blanche. Slowly, Amaria's breathing stabilized as they walked through the lit corridors.

"I wanted to spend time with you," Theodmon said. "I didn't mean to bring you in the dark. I forgot."

Amaria wrung her hands together. "It's alright," she choked out. Theodmon didn't seem as if he intended this action to be malicious.

"No," Theodmon said. "It's not." A long silence passed between the two.

Theodmon cast a furtive glance around the corridor, dropping his voice as he leaned in towards Amaria. "I'm scared of spiders."

Amaria raised her eyebrows. "You seem like such an outdoorsman."

"I like the other things," Theodmon laughed. "Not the spiders."

Amaria chuckled. "Thank you."

"For what?"

Amaria opened her hands slightly in front of her. "This. Being kind. Letting me know your fears," Amaria listed. "All of it. You've gone out of your way to welcome me here."

"I'm your husband," Theodmon chuckled.

"But most don't try to comfort their new wives. And you are. So thank you. I appreciate it more than you know."

Theodmon kissed the top of her head. "It's no issue."

She sighed, breathing in the smell of cedar and musk from his cologne, as she laid her head against his chest. This display of affection was entirely too public. Amaria could only imagine what the guards passing would say.

She could only imagine what her father would say if he knew. She had been given a second chance at marriage and she was already failing to meet the expectations of that.

"We should head to dinner," Theodmon said, pulling away. "We can only make the others wait so long until it's considered impolite."

Amaria gave a shaky chuckle, holding onto Theodmon's arm once more.

Theodmon whispered in her ear, his lips brushing across her skin. "I would like to embrace you more tonight after dinner."

Amaria's heart pounded as her hands gripped Theodmon's arm a bit more firmly. "I'd enjoy that."

Chapter Seven

"Nice to see you finally arrived," a stern looking woman said as Theodmon and Amaria entered the dining hall. Across from her, Aaron was drinking from his goblet.

"Not now, Mother." Theodmon's mouth thinned. Amaria's eyes widened slightly as she looked between them. "I'd like us all to enjoy dinner."

Theodmon's mother, Agatha Chauvignon's, eyebrows furrowed. "It is rude to be late-"

"And I've outgrown your lectures." Theodmon pulled out a chair for Amaria. Forcing back a lump in her throat, Amaria nodded towards him, smiling in gratitude.

"It is a pleasure to see you, Dowager Marchioness," Amaria said as a servant came and filled her goblet with wine.

Theodmon's mother's nostrils flared and she gave a humph. Amaria forced herself to remain composed, but she noticed her father's eyes narrowing.

"I hope there's beet soup," Celestine said cheerily. "I love beet soup."

"Because you're weird," Aloysius muttered under his breath.

"It's a northern delicacy," Juliette chuckled. "Or so everyone keeps telling me."

"How are you enjoying the north, Marchioness?" Lucas directed towards Amaria.

"I've not seen very much of it. I'm hoping the wedding tour will change that. The small amounts of the Westerlands I've been lucky enough to visit are gorgeous."

"I'm sure you've seen more of the northern hemisphere than the Westerlands," Agatha said, her voice as smooth as silk.

Amaria felt heat flush across her body. "I thought we were talking about the Westerlands specifically in this conversation."

"But there's more in the no-"

"Mother," Theodmon interrupted, his voice booming. "Not now."

"I apologize for any offense I may have caused," Amaria said. Despite not caring that she caused any offense, she knew it was the polite thing to say. She turned towards Celestine. "Please, would you tell me more about this soup?"

They all engaged in forced niceties, pretending there weren't brewing tensions until the main course. At this point, Aloysius was several glasses of mead in, and was on the brink of singing a drinking song.

"He's an awful singer," Lucas said, causing Aloysius's face to flush.

"No worse than I am, I'm sure." Amaria laughed behind her hand. "Apparently making milk curdle from the sound of your voice is the indication of a lack of talent and not a talent itself."

"Surely you can't be that bad," Juliette said.

Haerdnor snorted, choking on his drink. Amaria slowly turned her head towards him, her smile frozen on her face. This idiot. This rude idiot.

"She is." Nicoletta leaned forward, her eyes sparkling. "So bad that she was excused from all music lessons."

"And what were those lessons replaced with?" Agatha Chauvignon's eyes narrowed as if they were snake eyes.

"Dancing," Amaria said brightly, pretending as if she didn't see how Agatha was acting. "Thankfully, my grace in dancing makes up for my tone-deafness."

Agatha gave a hmph but said no more.

"Dowager Marchioness," Aaron said as he cut his venison with his knife. "What will you be doing with your spare time now? I'm sure you'll have more time to relax since you are being relieved of the duties of Lady of the Estate?"

"This venison is delicious," Celestine said, not breaking her eyes away from her mother. "Did one of you hunt it?" Her eyes flickered towards her brothers, however, she did not shift her direction away from her mother.

Henri chuckled into his wine. Amaria's eyebrows rose. What did he hear from one of their thoughts that was so amusing?

Aloysius smirked. "That buck tried to kill me."

"Shame he didn't succeed." Theodmon rolled his eyes. "Perhaps you wouldn't be as dramatic then."

Aloysius raised his goblet, grinning. "If dead people can't be dramatic, then explain ghosts."

Amaria took a small bite of her potatoes, washing it down with her wine, so she wouldn't burst out laughing at Aloysius's antics. Beside her, she noticed Theodmon's jaw twitched.

"Theodmon," she whispered, leaning in closer to him. "What's for desert?"

He chuckled under his breath. "You have a sweet tooth?"

"Only slightly."

"Chouquette," Theodmon informed her.

Amaria smiled. "That sounds lovely."

Soon the pastries, filled to the brim with chocolate mousse and sugar, arrived and the rest of the dinner went smoothly. Once everyone had a cup of tea, they departed. Amaria's head began to ring with fatigue.

"Dinner took too long," Theodmon whispered in Amaria's ear as they made their way back to their chambers.

"I enjoyed it," Amaria stated neutrally.

Theodmon snorted.

"I did," Amaria insisted. "The food was lovely. And I enjoyed most of the company."

"Most," Theodmon noted. "I apologize for my mother."

"I'm sure it must be difficult to lose your firstborn to marriage." Amaria did not care for Agatha or her behavior but it wasn't as if she could tell Theodmon that.

Theodmon shook his head. "It's not that. Don't give her that much credit–she hates you specifically."

"Why?" Amaria already knew the answer. Still, allowing Theodmon to explain things wouldn't harm her, and in fact might make him warm up to her.

"She's Morrian by birth. And she takes great offense to you and your father's actions in Morroek."

Amaria and her father had manipulated Morroek's economy to force manufactured famine's and then sold verta, an appetite suppressant, and limited food at an increased price to Morroek. They bought out anyone else who wished to sell grain to Morroek—the exercise didn't gain them money, in fact they only broke even. But Morroek becoming destabilized, festering for the empire to eventually take, was worth more than gold. Haerdnor and her father conducted a similar exercise in Rindria.

Of course someone from one of those nations would despise the Raulets. Amaria bit her lip, wishing her mother-in-law was anybody else.

"I don't know what to say."

Theodmon pulled her against him, looking fiercely in her eyes. The moonlight flooded in from the windows, illuminating him in an almost ethereal glow. "There's nothing to say."

"She's your mother. I don't want to cause any issue-"

"My mother will get over it. You're my wife." He leaned down and whispered in her ear. "Let's get to our chambers."

Amaria's dress suddenly felt heavy, too hot, and she needed to take it off. "Yes," she breathlessly agreed, breaking away from their embrace. Amaria's muscles tightened, her heartbeat thudding against her chest as Theodmon led them down the hall. This felt familiar, he had led her in a similar way only a few days prior. But then she had been terrified of sex, acting no better than a timid kitchen maid.

Now, she wasn't as scared, she knew what to expect and she had even found herself enjoying the act.

It had only been days, and while some things about the whole situation were unfamiliar and unnerving, Amaria found herself surprisingly comfortable in Theodmon's bed. She hadn't expected this to occur at her wedding, and even now, she suppressed the thought as if acknowledging it would make her circumstances change-as if her good luck would flee if she knew Amaria understood her fortune.

Amaria focused on the calluses on Theodmon's hands as he pulled her through the white stone corridors. He was strong. Amaria had seen him fight at tournaments before and she hoped he would use some of that strength with her.

Not now, of course. It would be crass to hope her husband would pick her up while he fucked her.

"Almost there." A smile tugged at the corner of Theodmon's lips. "Just give me a moment to greet the guards and give instructions for us not to be disturbed."

"May we have wine or mead brought up?" Amaria asked.

Theodmon's eyebrows raised. "Sure. Any reason on why?"

Amaria's face burned. "It'd be impolite to say."

Theodmon laughed, speeding up his gait, Amaria jogging to keep up with his long strides. It felt as if they were in the corridors for an eternity, but they stopped in front of the chamber doors.

Amaria bit her lip, looking downwards to hide the creeping smile upon her lips as Theodmon gave a curt greeting to the guards, giving them their instructions for the night. Once the guards acknowledged the commands, Theodmon pulled Amaria into their chambers, candles flickering brightly enough to illuminate the shadows around the floorboards.

As soon as the door thudded behind them, Theodmon pulled Amaria against him, his mouth pressing against hers as they kissed. She pulled him closer to her, her fingers interlocking through his hair. She smelled the soft woodsy scent, underlying spicy notes wafting from him. A sudden throbbing appeared near her groin, and she pressed her body closer to Theodmon's, wishing to be with him.

"Undress," Theodmon commanded. "Take out that braid."

Amaria laughed, undoing the twine at the end of her braid, slowly letting the long dark brown locks cascade down her back freely. She took off the overdress, the cloth tumbling to the floor.

Theodmon, now shirtless, came closer to her, pulling her back against his chest. His hands brushed against the strings of her dress as he untied her, his lips brushing against her neck. The hairs on her body rose, and she felt herself longing to turn around and pull Theodmon closer to her.

He kissed her neck and back as he pulled the unlaced dress off her shoulders. She breathed in heavily, her stomach fluttering, feeling herself become wet.

"I want you." Theodmon lips brushing over her ear. She gasped, turning herself around to look at him, pulling herself closer to his body. His trousers were still on and she was naked in front of him. Without breaking eye contact, she rubbed her hands over her breasts before moving her hands down to the strings at his trousers.

Amaria's hands fumbled over the strings. Theodmon pulled her in for a kiss, biting the lower part of her lip as his trousers fell to the ground.

"Come here. Let me carry you." He didn't wait for a response, picking her up with her legs wrapped around him. "I'm going to fuck you against the wall."

Amaria moaned, pushing her body closer against his as he propped her against the wall, inserting himself easily. Her entire body tingled, she needed him inside of her. He fiercely pounded himself inside, and her hands clawed at his back.

This was perfect. This was euphoria.

She screamed, her naked body being pounded against the stone walls. Amaria pulled herself closer to him as she gave off a soft whimper.

"You like that?"

Amaria laid her head on his shoulder. She liked being with him, having him inside her. He pounded himself against her and she closed her eyes, sighing. All she wanted was this, no matter how long this lasted.

Theodmon kissed her neck as she gripped his member with her insides. "You're beautiful," he said, the hairs on her neck raising as she moaned. She tightened her embrace around him, leaning her head back as she gave a breathy sigh.

She would be alright if life began and ended right here.

Chapter Eight

Amaria blinked, pulling the heavy blankets over her face as the sun shined through the windows as she stretched.

"Good morning," Theodmon said.

Amaria turned her head to look at him, meeting his hazel eyes. He had flecks of blue in them, as if his eyes were a driftwood fire spark in the middle of honey.

He pulled her closer to him. "How'd you sleep?"

Amaria yawned, snuggling closer to him. She didn't know him well, but for some reason she felt comforted by his presence.

"Well enough."

"I've called for breakfast," Theodmon said.

Amaria's eyebrows rose. "Breakfast?"

"The meal you eat in the morning? Don't you have that in Raulle?"

"Of course." Amaria pulled away from Theodmon as she sat up in bed. "But in our rooms?"

Theodmon looked at her quizzically as he sat up with her. "Where did you eat breakfast?"

"The great hall."

Theodmon made a choking sound. "Every day?"

Amaria wrapped her arms around herself. "My father never let me have breakfast in my rooms."

"Do you want to have breakfast in the great hall?"

Amaria bit her lip. She hadn't ever thought about where she'd prefer to have breakfast. She just ate where she was expected to. What would it be like to not having to dress before having a slice of toast? "Breakfast here would be nice."

"What do you usually have for breakfast?" Theodmon asked.

"Fruits, bread, some seafood like crab, tuna, caviar." Amaria shrugged. "What do you eat here?"

"Bread, bacon, eggs, fruit. I'm sure if you wanted, we could add some salmon to breakfast."

Amaria smiled. "That's kind of you." She breathed in deeply, catching sight of the crumbled embroidery thread kicked into the basket in the corner. She would have to work on that tapestry more.

"What are you doing today?"

"Final preparations for our wedding tour. I'm sorry it's taking so long to leave...." Theodmon trailed off with a heavy sigh.

Amaria turned to look Theodmon directly in his eyes, taking in their calculating gaze, how they seemed to shift around the room, as if looking for threats. "I want to know more about you."

Theodmon laughed. "What do you want to know?"

Everything. Amaria met Theodmon's eyes, determined to say something that wasn't as pathetic as that thought. She was clever, she should be able to think of a clever question.

"What's your favorite fruit?"

She stopped herself from cringing as she asked that question.

"Apples," Theodmon said. "You?"

"Lemons," Amaria said. "Sometimes pomegranates."

"Southerner," Theodmon scoffed, unable to hide his smile.

"When I was a child there was a pomegranate tree at Provincia Palencia...." Amaria said wistfully, staring ahead at the wall as she twirled her hair around her fingers.

"Did you get stuck climbing it?"

"Gods no, do you know how small that tree was? That'd be pathetic."

"So what's the childhood story then?"

A knock rapped outside.

"One moment," Theodmon said, swinging himself out of bed. Amaria followed, stretching and moving over to the small table in the room as Theodmon brought in trays with the help of the servants.

Amaria poured herself and Theodmon a cup of tea. "When we were all born, my mother had a dwarf tree planted for us in the gardens: Orange for Haerdnor, lemon for me, pomegranate for Catalina." She picked up a sugar cube, dunking it into her tea. "Catalina hates pomegranates."

"Ironic."

Amaria chuckled in agreement as she stirred her tea. "She grew to appreciate it, after...." Amaria trailed off, her mouth turning dry. *After Mother died.* "Catalina hated this tree, so Haerdnor taunted her with it, throwing his orange peels at her."

"Typical," Theodmon dryly said, as he cut into the sausage the plate in front of him. "Where does the tree come in?"

"I'm getting there," Amaria promised before taking a small bite of the pastry in front of her. "Have you ever heard of fire ants?"

"Of course. What did Haerdnor do?"

"Haerdnor?" Amaria scoffed. "Who said Haerdnor did anything? No, Catalina and I did this."

Theodmon inclined his head. "What did you and your sister do?"

"Well, I convinced Haerdnor it would be a wonderful prank if we picked all the pomegranates from Catalina's trees and instead hung baskets of lemons and oranges from the branches. Meanwhile, Catalina and I were wondering if fire ants would burn a fire mage."

"And you were unwilling to sacrifice yourself for the experiment?" Theodmon's eyes twinkled.

Amaria smirked, her eyes twinkling. "I used my wind magic to have bags of fire ants floating in the trees as Haerdnor picked the fruit-I couldn't do it because it would be horribly unladylike to climb trees-especially when my father had ambassadors visiting."

"And when the bags mysteriously fell down?"

"Turns out fire mages are only immune to actual flames. A noble sacrifice on Haerdnor's part. And he was sadly bedridden, and the ambassadors were so looking forward to meeting my father's eldest son, it was a shame I was introduced instead."

Theodmon looked at her for a long while. "And how old were you when this happened?"

"Mother was still alive, perhaps six or so."

"Six and already scheming to be in the room where decisions were made," Theodmon raised his glass towards her. "Unusual, but I can respect it."

"I've mellowed since then," Amaria said.

"I sincerely doubt it. But, I'm glad. You intrigue me, Amaria. I think we'll be quite a team if we work together."

"Of course," Amaria agreed, unsure of what else to say.

"Please don't take this the wrong way." Theodmon rolled his neck. "But was this around the time you became your father's creature?"

"My father's creature?" Amaria questioned.

"You were an extension of him, no?" Theodmon said. "In conducting his affairs."

Amaria shrugged. "I'd like to think I had my own agency, but in that I helped manage his affairs, yes I was an extension of him."

"Would you like to continue to manage those types of affairs?"

Amaria looked at him, her eyes widening. "Economic?" she asked, not wanting to admit to the other dirty work. It was crass, and she didn't need to scare her husband away from her so early.

"And others." Theodmon leaned closer to her. "I've heard you're an adept torturer."

Amaria watched him, searching for a sign of disapproval or disgust. "Would it bother you if that rumor was true?"

"No," Theodmon said. "But it's a skill I'd want you to utilize here. May I be honest with you?"

Amaria's mouth was as dry as if she'd fallen face first into sand.

"I didn't marry you because of your dowry or because it'd be nice to have a beautiful wife in bed."

Amaria scoffed.

"It's true," Theodmon said. "I married you because I want power, and your connections help, but also your skill set. You're different from most noble ladies—I don't want to spurn those skills."

Amaria squeezed Theodmon's hand. "Me either."

Theodmon sighed. "I should head out." He cast a dark look towards the door. "Let's have dinner in our chambers?"

The two of them dressed and Amaria mournfully watched Theodmon shovel down the last of his sausages before striding towards the exit of their rooms.

"What's your favorite gemstone?" Theodmon asked as he departed.

Amaria bit her lip as she surveyed Theodmon. "Would it be too expected if I said sapphire?"

He chuckled. "Perhaps. Maybe a non-expected stone?"

Amaria picked at her nails as she ran through a list of gemstones. She dismissed rubies, that would make her seem like a sycophant. She hated amethysts. Perhaps aquamarine? Emerald? She felt as if she would pull the skin off her thumbnail before she could think of something adequate.

She liked pearls. But perhaps he expected that from her as well. He seemed as if wanted something more unusual than the commonly gifted gemstones.

She smiled, lifting her eyes to meet his as she realized what she wanted. "Black pearl."

Chapter Nine

Amaria didn't stay in her chambers once Theodmon left. Instead, she started searching for her brother, desperate to spend a few last moments with him. There couldn't be too many places he'd be and this would give her an excuse to explore Forteresse les Blanche by herself. She appreciated Theodmon showing her around, but she felt overwhelmed at times by it. She was an outsider and him explaining centuries of history made that even more evident.

She could have given a similar tour at Provincia Palencia, but she wouldn't be able to. Not anymore.

She searched for Haerdnor in the kitchens, in his chambers, at the great hall, and she found him at the stables.

"Haerdnor?"

Haerdnor turned around, his arms crossed. "Yes?"

"What are you doing here?"

"I'm here for your wedding." Haerdnor smirked. "Is the mountain air deluding-"

"I meant the stables," Amaria interrupted, rolling her eyes.

"The horses are fantastic." Haerdnor's eyes lit up. "These war stallions might be more well bred than ours." He launched into a monologue on the specifics on each stallion. Amaria zoned out, unable to keep up. She had never paid attention to horses. "Why are you here?"

"Hmm?"

"Why are you here?" Haerdnor repeated. "I know you aren't here for the horses. Where's Theodmon? Are you lost?" He gave her a fake pout.

Amaria crossed her arms. "I was looking for you. I know you're leaving soon, I wanted to spend some time with you before I don't see you for gods' knows how long."

Haerdnor held up his hands, walking away from the stables. Her arms still crossed, Amaria followed him. In truth, she was thankful they were leaving the stables. It smelled disgusting near the horses.

Amaria and Haerdnor walked around the mountain path, the birds flying high above. They didn't need to say anything to understand and enjoy each other. Gods, Amaria was going to miss him. She loved her twin, and while they'd gone months apart–she didn't know how long it would be before she saw him again.

"Do you like it here?" Haerdnor asked.

Amaria sighed, staring out into the horizon. "I can't answer that. I barely know my way around this estate-it's too new."

"Fine," Haerdnor conceded. "Do you think you'll like it here?"

A slight smile tugged at the corners of Amaria's lips. "I might. It's too early to say for sure."

They passed a small stone bench, ivy growing along the top of it. Amaria summoned her magic, dispelling the ivy to shift and wrap itself around the legs of the bench.

"You'll terrify the gardeners," Haerdnor said. "They're going to have the shock of their lives."

"What do you mean by that?" Amaria sat down on the bench, looking over the mountains.

"You're a neurotic monster."

"I'm not that bad."

Haerdnor snorted as he sat next to her. "You gave your last maid nightmares."

Amaria rolled her eyes. "Stop exaggerating." She laid her head on Haerdnor's shoulder. "I'm going to miss you."

She felt his shoulders rise as he inhaled. "Me too. It's just me at home now. Catalina is at a temple and you're gone–"

"You can have all of our rooms," Amaria joked.

Haerdnor chuckled. "My next room change will be when Father departs for Sadthos's silent kingdom." He shook his head. "Let's not talk about this. I don't want to be sad. I don't want this to be more painful than it already is."

Amaria wrapped her arms around herself. "What about a mage duel? One last one."

"As long as you use water. I don't think destroying your husband's ancestral home is wise."

Amaria hit his arm with the back of her hand, laughing. "Fine."

For the next few hours, they played with their magic. Neither truly dueled each other–it couldn't even be described as a training duel. They were just spending time together, using their magic as a shield to avoid facing their thoughts.

As the sun started setting, Amaria and Haerdnor headed back down to the castle, Theodmon stopping them when they neared the stables.

Theodmon gave Haerdnor a short bow of his head. "Lord Raulet." He turned towards Amaria, extending his hand to her. "Amaria, would you mind accompanying me?"

"I'll leave you to it." Haerdnor gave Amaria a slight squeeze on her arm before he departed.

Amaria looked upwards at Theodmon. "Where are we going?"

"I'm showing you more of your home before subjecting you to more dinners."

Amaria's throat tightened. "I thought we were having a private dinner?"

"We are." Theodmon squeezed her hand. "Ah...that was a bad joke."

"No," Amaria lied. "It wasn't that bad."

For hours, they walked around the grounds as Theodmon showed her more of the estate. He pointed out different paintings, tapestries and suits of armor to her, explaining their history. Amaria's eyes glazed over after an hour of this, but still, she followed him.

Theodmon paused in the foyer near the courtyard. "What do you think?"

"There're so many suits of armor."

Theodmon chuckled. "I suppose that's true."

Amaria smiled at him. "Thank you for showing me around."

He took her hand in his. "Let me show you the gardens. Then we can go to our chambers."

"Marquis." A woman with long, curly blonde hair came up to them, twirling a strand of pearls.

Theodmon took a slight step backwards, his body tensing. Amaria could see a muscle protruding in his neck.

"Lady Maiges. This is my wife, Marchioness Chauvignon."

Lady Maiges bit her lip, looking Amaria up and down. "I thought you liked blondes." She looked at Theodmon with childlike wide blue eyes.

Theodmon stepped closer to Amaria as he glared at Livia. "Stop."

Amaria felt as if a knife was plunged into her heart. Livia Maiges. The rumors said she was Theodmon's long time mistress. And Livia was still around. Would Theodmon run back to her? Would he tire of Amaria? Was he already tired of Amaria?

"I would have hoped to be introduced to your wife earlier," Livia said. "As she is the mistress of this house. I'm sure she'll be different from your mother or Celestine."

Theodmon's mouth tensed. "It was unfortunate you were sick and couldn't attend the wedding. You could have met Marchioness Chauvignon with the rest of the world."

Livia gave a small frown.

Amaria couldn't breathe. She needed to leave this situation before she started crying or yelling. Tears formed in her eyes. "My Lord Husband," she said with a curtsy. "If you would excuse me."

"Amaria," Theodmon said.

Amaria was already departing, trying to push back the bile coming up. She would go to her chambers and lock herself away from the world. Anything to pretend she hadn't met Theodmon's mistress.

As she departed, Amaria heard the final snippets of their conversation. She paused, dipping behind a column, despite every instinct telling her it was best not to know.

Livia stepped closer to Theodmon. "I'm still around."

Theodmon stepped away, his hands in front of him as if he were about to push her away. "It's over, Livia. I have a wife."

Livia snorted. "And you care about honor? I wish you cared about that before you brought me to your bed for years."

"You came willingly. I never asked you to come to me. Livia, you started this."

"And you enjoyed it." Livia twirled a strand of hair. "I'm still available, if she ever bores you. Wives can be tedious, right?"

"You test the bounds of my charity," Theodmon said. "You insult me or my wife again and there will be consequences. I care for you, but whatever we had is over."

Amaria bit her lip, stifling a sob. Why was she upset? He was picking her over his mistress? But what if he changed? mind? Her position wasn't secured here. Not yet, anyways.

She picked up the hem of her skirt and walked through the halls, wishing she could run without gossip following. She had to get to her chambers. She had to have privacy.

Livia Maiges was a thorn in a wound she didn't even know she had. And Amaria wanted her gone. But she didn't have the power here. All she could do was play her role, and slowly make Theodmon amenable to her wishes.

Maybe one day Livia would be away from Forteresse les Blanche. And maybe, once that day occurred, Amaria would feel secure. Until then, she would be a good wife and cement her place in this court.

Chapter Ten

"It's coming along." Nicoletta peered over Amaria's shoulder as she pulled a needle though the union tapestry. Two of the borders had been completed, and Amaria was growing tired of gold, red, and forest green thread.

"Hardly," Amaria said. She likely wouldn't finish the borders before she and Theodmon left for their wedding tour. She'd spent the last four days sewing in her chambers, waiting for Theodmon to finish his business so they could depart. Amaria jabbed her needle through the fabric, roughly pulling it through, biting her lip.

She had to finish it. It knew it was stupid, but meeting Livia Maiges had unnerved her. And how Theodmon had so readily admitted she had been his mistress for years....

Amaria's throat constricted as she remembered how Theodmon didn't even try to save face.

"Most women take a whole year to complete these." Juliette peered over at Amaria's handiwork. "You have time."

Amaria placed her sewing down. "I want to get the border done before I leave."

"Are you packed for your tour?" Nicoletta asked.

Amaria wasn't even sure if she was unpacked from moving here yet, let alone ready for the month-long trip around the Westerlands. She shrugged. "I'll ask the servants."

"It's been done," Juliette said. "I've checked. They're already loaded in the carriage."

Amaria turned around to look at Juliette, her eyebrows raising.

"What?" Juliette gave a small shrug. "I like to organize."

"Some would call you neurotic." Nicoletta crossed her arms with a huff. "You know I'm the principal lady-in-waiting-"

"Yes," Amaria said soothingly. "You are. But you just moved here and Juliette is helping us both get settled in." She looked over at Juliette. "Do you know if the raspberry leaves are packed?"

"I'll place them in the carry on," Juliette said.

"So soon?" Nicoletta asked. "You were just married. Can't you wait a few months longer before actively trying?"

"I want to cement myself as soon as possible." Amaria cast Nicoletta a dark look. "A son does that."

Besides, what would waiting do? Noblewomen were expected to deliver multiple children–heir, spares, and daughters to marry off for alliances. Amaria would rather face what was expected instead of fleeing from it, cowering in fear of inevitability.

Before Juliette or Nicoletta could respond, the door opened, revealing Theodmon.

Juliette and Nicoletta rose, curtsying to him. Amaria tilted her head, lifting her eyes demurely to observe him. He had sweat along his brow, and a loose curl hung down over his forehead. His hazel eyes were striking–they shouldn't have been as they were a common enough color, but something in Theodmon's gaze captivated her.

"Leave," he commanded the two others.

"My Lord," Nicoletta muttered as she departed.

"Lady Bécharil," Theodmon called out, causing Juliette to turn.

"Yes, Marquis?" Juliette asked.

"Prepare Lucas to help Aloysius run Forteresse les Blanche while I'm gone."

"Of course," Juliette replied with one last curtsy before she departed, the door shutting with a thud behind her.

"Your brother doesn't run Forteresse les Blanche alone?"

"He's too much of a drunkard," Theodmon snorted. "Besides, Lucas is my right hand. He's aware of what's occurring and can ensure everything doesn't go to shit-even if Aloysius is high on verta."

Amaria's eyebrows rose, unsure of what to say. She knew that Aloysius did the drug; rumors flew and considering her family had a near monopoly on the drug-she'd seen his name in her ledgers.

Theodmon moved to sit beside her. "We're having dinner soon and we should then get some rest. We're leaving tomorrow."

"Really?" Amaria beamed.

"We should leave at dawn-"

"Could we leave later in the day? I'd like to visit Chauvi before we leave and I've been avoiding the city because I wanted you to show me."

Theodmon's hand cupped her jaw, and she felt her face being raised to meet his. He kissed her and her eyes shut as she tilted her head back.

"Of course. We'll leave for Chauvi at nine in the morning and have breakfast in the markets."

"Can we talk?"

"About what?"

Amaria wet her lips. "Livia."

Theodmon's shoulder slumped. "There's nothing between us–"

"She was your mistress for years."

"And now she's not. What would you have me do? She's minor nobility and her past with me makes her unmarriageable–she doesn't have the connections you do to overcome that. I'm not leaving her destitute."

Amaria's face flushed. "I'm not suggesting that!"

"Then what are you saying? You'd love to send her away, wouldn't you? To make sure I don't stray?"

Amaria recoiled. She would love for Livia Maiges to not exist around Theodmon, he wasn't incorrect there, but the intensity of how he said it shocked her."

"We could pay for her maintenance," Amaria whispered. "A country estate–"

"Until you're suspicious of the amount of money being sent. I've seen this pattern happen in my court before."

"What if I got her a new position? A better position than your mistress."

Theodmon snorted. "I'm listening."

"My cousin, the emperor, has multiple mistresses. My father, he can put in a good word for her. Aion owes him. I'd never suggest leaving her destitute, but please, wouldn't this benefit everyone?"

Theodmon slumped back in his chair, surveying her. Amaria's heart thudded. She didn't know what would happen if he said no. She played her hand incorrectly, she didn't have this influence over Theodmon. Most wives tolerated their husband's mistresses, she should have done the same.

Theodmon ran a hand through his hair. "Write to your father. If Aion accepts her as a mistress, I'll send her away. I'm sure she wouldn't mind the upgrade. But if he doesn't, you'll have to tolerate her and trust me when I say it is only you. Please don't be jealous of my past." Theodmon kissed her on the lips. "You are my present and future."

Amaria gingerly nodded, unsure of how else to respond.

"Now rest," Theodmon said. "We have a long journey ahead."

Chapter Eleven

"Have you ever been to Chauvi?" Theodmon asked Amaria as he led her through the morning markets.

"Once, for your father's funeral." She didn't remember much of that day or of Chauvi, as she'd been around ten years old. Next to her, Theodmon tensed. "I'm sorry for bringing it up, I know it's difficult to lose a parent."

Theodmon stared ahead. Amaria resisted wringing her hands, her heart thumping as she held her hands together under her lavender sleeves. She ruined their nice morning. She shouldn't have said anything.

"It's difficult. But life goes on."

Amaria breathed a sigh of relief as Theodmon turned to point towards a few tents.

"Those have the most wonderful croissants," he said. "They bake them fresh and bring them to market daily. And there's custard in them."

"I'm more partial to jams." Amaria linked her arm with Theodmon's. "What else do they have at this market?"

"Flowers, baubles, armor, food, wine, beer, mead, knives, perfume–anything you could imagine. Are you looking for something in particular?"

Amaria turned her head to take in the bustling city, with merchants shouting their wares. Chauvi wasn't as large as Raulle, nor as hectic, but Amaria enjoyed it. She felt a peace as she looked over at the mountains and the evergreens pressing against the city. "I was just curious."

"I hate that you missed the annual boat races," Theodmon said. "Every year there's a race on the lake with boats made by hand, but no actual sailor or boat craftsman can take part. So you'll have a baker, a blacksmith, a soldier, a jeweler–all of them are trying to make a half decent boat and win."

Amaria laughed. "That sounds delightful."

Theodmon paused near a table lined with flowers. "There's a monetary prize, so the citizens get competitive." He moved closer to the florists booth. "How much for a bouquet?"

Amaria blushed, feeling her heart flutter. "That isn't necessary," she muttered, more out of social politeness than the hope he would not buy her flowers.

"Four crowns," the florist said, and Theodmon handed over four small bronze coins.

"My Lord." The florist nodded her head in thanks as she handed him a bouquet filled with powder blue delphinium, bright pink stonecrop, vibrant purple mountain laurel, and bright yellow honeysuckle.

It was unlike any other bouquet Amaria had received before. "They're beautiful." She cast a small smile towards the florist as well, including her in the compliment.

They departed from the florist, stopping at a baker's stall to have breakfast, eating donuts filled with custard. Afterwards, they meandered through the market, pausing at stalls to inspect the wares, smelling the perfumes and holding the baubles in the sunlight, laughing.

"That blacksmith is phenomenal," Theodmon told Amaria as they passed a tent filled to the brim with armor, swords, and arrows.

"Do you want to go look?"

"We can look at things you're more familiar with."

"I've held a dagger before." Amaria looked at him pointedly. "In the Drowning Tombs."

"I suppose you have." Theodmon chuckled. "Alright, let's go." They made their way to the blacksmith, Theodmon and him launching into a detailed discussion of weaponry upon arrival.

As the men talked, Amaria wandered around the table, looking at the wares for sale. In the corner of her eye, she caught a flash of red sparkling in the sunlight and turned to see a jeweled dagger, its hilt polished gold and ruby, the metal sanded down until it was smooth. She moved closer to the dagger, gingerly picking it up.

It was heavy. Amaria balanced the blade in her hand, the gold and rubies caressing her palm. The knife was beautiful, from the fleur de lis hilt, and the golden and onyx swirl, bird, and floral inlays in the blade itself, matching the intricate metal sheath.

"Do you want it?" Theodmon asked, appearing close to her. Amaria could tell he was looking at the blade from over her shoulder.

"Yes." Amaria was unable to hide her desire behind social expectations. She wasn't supposed to want a dagger, but she did. But she also wasn't supposed to visit dungeons regularly, and yet she did that. Besides, courts could be dangerous places. "A sheath for my leg too. I want to hide it under my skirts."

"I'll have it ordered and waiting for you once we return home." Theodmon turned to the blacksmith, exchanging the coins for the dagger and writing out an order for Amaria's sheath that the blacksmith would deliver to the tanner as he had the measurements of the dagger.

"I hope you enjoy, Marchioness," the blacksmith said.

Amaria inclined her head. "It is beautiful work."

And once she had her sheath, Amaria intended on always having the dagger on her person. Her magic was frightening and could protect her well enough, but there was something satisfying in cutting someone open as if they were a sow.

She looked at the dagger again, finding beauty in the gold, red, and black. "Thank you," she told Theodmon, tears appearing in her eyes as they departed from the blacksmith.

He squeezed her hand as he looked around the market. "Are you ready to depart for the rest of our tour? There's more to the city, but we can see more of that in the years we live at Forteresse les Blanche."

Amaria nodded, her mouth turning dry as her face flushed. "Yes, of course," she said, stumbling over her own words. "Where is the carriage?"

Anything to get Theodmon speaking. She despised that she was so flustered. Why was she this way now? She had never been this timid.

Theodmon chuckled, leading her through the city to the carriage. Amaria was surprisingly tired, as soon as they were in the carriage, she felt her eyes becoming heavy. The trees and mountains flashed past them as they drove outside the city. The carriage rocked slightly and Amaria rested her head against Theodmon's shoulder.

"Sleep," he cooed, brushing his hands over her hair. "We've a while until we reach the next stop."

Crickets chirped in the trees outside as Amaria's eyes slowly fluttered open, the light from dusk pouring into the carriage through the windows. She rolled her neck as she sat up, getting the cricks out.

"Enjoy your nap?" Theodmon asked.

Amaria rubbed her eyes. "I don't know why I was so tired."

"You came from Raulle a few weeks ago. Surely you weren't ready to travel more?"

Amaria shrugged. "Perhaps. Where are we now?"

"We're nearing Dovesport. We'll stop there for the night."

"Isn't Dovesport near the faeries' lands?"

"It's where I meet with them as the liaison," Theodmon confirmed. "And they're why we're stopping for the night. The fae are volatile and unpredictable."

"Even to you as the liaison?"

"Especially to me," Theodmon scowled. "Oberon-that's the faerie I primarily meet with-seems to have made it his immortal life's mission to aggravate me."

Amaria's eyebrows rose. "It can't be that bad."

Theodmon shook his head. "He gets under my skin. It's hard to explain how-he's infuriating. You have to experience it to understand."

Amaria shrugged. "I believe you." As she shifted in her seat she kicked her bag, knocking it over, a vial of herbs and a few earrings falling out onto the carriage ground. Groaning, she leaned over to pick them up.

"What's the vial?"

"Fertility herbs," Amaria answered, pausing to sit up and open the cork. "Well a potion created with them." She lifted the vial upwards, intending to drink when Theodmon placed his hand over hers.

"Why so early? We just got married. I want to spend more time together. You're my wife–"

"And therefore it is my duty to provide you with heirs. I appreciate your kind words, Theodmon, I really do, but we have forever to get to know each other better–we are bound by the gods until death."

"I want our marriage to be more than-"

"Mere duties, yes," Amaria interrupted softly. "I want that as well. But I need security as well and these duties will provide that for me. If you were to die without a son I would return to my father and he would likely remarry me–I don't want that to happen."

Or, if he casted her aside for Livia, a son would secure her position regardless of how Theodmon's affections swayed.

Amaria's heart pounded in her chest as she clenched her jaw shut to prevent biting or licking her lips. This wasn't an easy conversation and she didn't want to challenge Theodmon so directly this early in the marriage.

Theodmon released her hand as he slumped back in his seat. "Alright."

Amaria's eyebrows rose before she composed herself, merging her face back into a neutral expression. She met Theodmon's eyes as she brought the vial to her lips, drinking the bitter drink within.

"How far away are we from Dovesport?" Amaria corked the bottle and dropped it in her bag.

"Likely an hour or so."

"Where are we staying? An inn?"

Theodmon chuckled, moving closer to Amaria. "Gods, no. I have a hunting lodge on the outskirts of the city."

"Do you hunt near the faerie lands often?"

"No." Theodmon pushed her hair back as he kissed her neck. "But with how often I travel to Dovesport an inn would be impractical." Amaria's skin tingled, feeling Theodmon's fingers dance over her back. "I can't wait."

"In the carriage?" Amaria questioned. "Are we sure that's wise?"

"Who will say anything?" Theodmon's hands ran up her legs, moving her skirts out of the way. "You're a married woman on her wedding tour." Amaria felt him push open her legs, stroking her inner thighs with his palms. "And you're trying to give me an heir, are you not?"

Amaria sighed, tilting her head back. "Yes," she said breathily.

"There's no reason both of us can't enjoy ourselves while we work on that." Theodmon inserted two of his fingers inside her.

She gasped as he moved his fingers up and down, feeling herself become wetter. They shouldn't be doing this, not in the carriage.

Amaria cupped her hands around Theodmon's face, forcing her lips against him, pulling him closer to her. Their lips clung together softly at first, then with more urgency-she needed him to breathe.

His fingers came out from inside her, and he was embracing her, pulling her closer, lifting up her skirts and undoing his trousers. The air inside the carriage was humid, uncomfortably so, beads of sweat appearing on Amaria's forehead.

"You're beautiful," Theodmon whispered in her ear.

She should accept the compliment, her husband complimenting her beauty while they engaged in intercourse shouldn't bother her–it should be an expected exchange. And it was, in part. But she still was bitter against that compliment as it seemed as if that was often the only thing that mattered about her.

He doesn't mean anything by it. Amaria tilted her head, exposing her neck more for Theodmon to kiss as he climbed on top of her, inserting himself. She thought Theodmon was handsome, and was even rubbing her hands over his biceps.

She sighed, her body relaxing. Amaria embraced him as they kissed, her fingernails digging into his back as Theodmon pulled her closer to him. Rhythmically, he pounded himself inside of her. She got wetter, dripping over him.

Amaria's back arched as she moaned. She didn't want this to end, but she slumped over on him, exhausted, as he pounded against her furiously, her fingers digging into his back. She shut her eyes, taking in the cedar scent of his cologne.

And then, she felt something run inside of her. Amaria's chest heaved as she collapsed in her seat, her head spinning. Her face felt hot and she had the sudden desire to pull her fan out of her bag to fan herself.

"Good?" Amaria asked as Theodmon pulled away from her, collapsing on the carriage seat across from her. He laid on his back as he panted, his hands on his chest.

For a few minutes, they sat in silence, composing themselves. And then, the carriage seemed to be slowing. The carriage stopped and the coachman threw open the doors.

"Oh gods," Amaria gasped, holding her dress in front of her to cover herself.

Theodmon threw his cloak over Amaria, her hair and corset still in slight disarray.

"Welcome to my Dovesport hunting lodge," Theodmon said as they stepped out of the carriage, Amaria catching sight of a modest stone building. "Maybe one day I'll bring you hunting here."

Amaria squeezed his hand. "I'd enjoy that."

Theodmon chuckled. "If I had known that, I would have brought supplies and we could have gone on this tour. Unfortunately, we're only staying the night here."

Amaria's eyes twinkled. "We have our entire marriage to come back."

Chapter Twelve

From Dovesport they traveled down to Adanes, skirting the edges of the Faerielands. Amaria, as they traveled, stared at the trees, almost hazy in a magical fog, in morbid fascination. She was apprehensive, but she could feel the magic and even from this distance it felt overpowering.

It felt intoxicating. For a moment, Amaria wondered what it would be like to have a taste of the faeries' power. And then, in a breath, that thought was gone. Everyone knew the fae were volatile and these thoughts were deluded ideas of grandeur that would never, and should never, occur.

As Amaria stared out her window, she talked with Theodmon. She was enjoying his company and she found him to be kind, charming, and intelligent.

She felt drawn to his presence.

When they were about a day outside of Adanes, headed to Monsa, Theodmon pulled out a stack of cards from his rucksack. "Do you know how to play?" He shuffled the cards in his hands.

"Depends on the game." Amaria leaned forward. "Which one are you thinking of?"

Theodmon began to deal out the cards. "Gin rummy."

Amaria burst into laughter. "Of course I know how to play gin rummy. I thought you were going to say something obscure like spite and malice."

"You've played spite and malice?" Theodmon's eyebrows rose.

"It's my father's favorite game," Amaria explained, forcing herself to ignore the sudden pang in her chest. "It's strategic, my father thought it would be a good exercise."

"Forgive me." Theodmon inclined his head towards her. "I didn't mean to insult you."

"Do you know how to play?"

"Vaguely." Theodmon blinked rapidly. "It was my father's favorite game-I've not played since...."

Theodmon trailed off, staring outside his window. Amaria noticed that his eyes seemed blank, as if he were no longer mentally in the carriage with her. Allowing him to sit in silence for a few moments, Amaria reached out and squeezed his hands. "Gin rummy it is."

For hours, they played cards. They played cards throughout the rest of the trip stopping only for food, rest, and sex. Not that Amaria minded. Sex, once a terrifying concept, was now enjoyable, pleasurable even. And she was growing to care about Theodmon.

She had been embarrassed when they arrived at Monsa and the footman inadvertently opened the door to see her licking cum off Theodmon's cock. While the footman had immediately shut the carriage door and Theodmon assured her nobody would think anything of a married woman acting that way with her husband, Amaria's face burned. That was a private moment and it had been infringed upon.

"I never want that footman with a carriage I'm in," she told Theodmon as they ensured they both were dressed.

"He won't say anything."

Amaria crossed her arms. "I'm mortified!"

Theodmon held up his hands as if in defeat. "I'll ensure that after this tour he will never be stationed with any carriage you travel in." He leaned down and kissed her on the mouth, tugging at her lip with his teeth. "Now, let me show you Monsa. There's a private lake outside the city that is better than anything you'd find within."

"Your estate?"

"Technically one of Aloysius's," Theodmon admitted. "But he's not there."

And he's a second son and you're the head of the family, so if you wanted to be cruel it could be yours again. Amaria smiled at Theodmon. She was glad he gave his siblings property. She was glad he wasn't cruel.

"I can't wait to see this lake," Amaria told Theodmon as he pulled her around the city walls, almost running towards the castle on a distant hill.

Theodmon's eyes sparkled as he pulled her through the fields. Amaria threw her head back, laughing as she sprinted to keep up with him. They made it to the castle, Amaria doubled over herself, panting, as Theodmon spoke to the guards and ensured their safe entry within.

"There's a pier." Theodmon grabbed her hands and brought her through the castle. "My siblings and I used to jump off it when we were children." He met her eyes, grinning. "Let's go swimming."

"Now?" It was a beautiful day, the sun was out and shining, a few clouds lingering in the sky. But she wasn't expecting this.

"It's summer!" Theodmon held her hands in his own. "I'll ensure we have privacy. It'll be fun."

Amaria smiled, twirling a strand of her dark hair as he pulled her into a sprint.

They ran through the gardens, stopping outside the lake, the waters a deep blue. It wasn't the crystalline waters of the sea outside Raulle, but Amaria admitted it was beautiful in its own way. Theodmon let go of her hand to take off his shirt and boots and then sprinted towards the pier, jumping off and curling his body into a ball until she hit the water, an explosive splash coming from it.

Amaria followed, laughing, pulling off her outer clothes and shoes before sitting at the end of the pier, her feet dipping into the water. It was cold, but in the warm summer it felt good.

Theodmon swam up to her and held her hands. Before she could say or do anything, he pulled her into the lake.

Amaria shrieked as she fell into the water, coughing once her head bobbed above the surface.

Theodmon laughed. "I'll race you to the buoy."

"And you think I have a chance at winning?" Amaria raised an eyebrow. Theodmon was athletic and she wasn't.

Theodmon shrugged, his shoulders barely breaking the surface of the lake. "You're a water mage."

"That doesn't help with racing!" Amaria protested, laughing.

"On the count of ten. One, two, three...."

Amaria listened to him counting to ten, narrowing her eyes at the buoy in the distance. She was going to lose, she couldn't outrace him. Perhaps she could freeze the water around him so he couldn't move then break the ice once she was about to touch the buoy?

No. She liked him. What harm would losing once do? She'd swim her best and accept she would lose to him.

"...ten," Theodmon said, and Amaria started swimming, holding her breath as she swung her arms over her head. She didn't even notice that Theodmon hadn't even begun swimming until she stopped at the buoy, breathing heavily.

What? Her eyebrows scrunched together. She raised her hands, freezing a path of water in front of herself, pulling herself onto the icy bridge and walked over the lake to Theodmon.

"Why didn't you race?" Amaria questioned, releasing her magic so the ice melted back into the lake and standing next to Theodmon, the warm water lapping around them.

"You were distracting. I forgot to swim."

Amaria snorted. "I'm distracting?"

"Yes, do you see yourself?"

"Well, no. There isn't a mirror."

Theodmon gave a sarcastic laugh at the joke.

"Don't give me that kind of laugh." Amaria crossed her arms. "It was funny." She wrung the water from her hair. "Why'd you let me win?"

"Because I might love you."

Amaria had no response to that. After all, she didn't freeze the lake around him for a similar reason.

Chapter Thirteen

A maria and Theodmon only spent a few days in Monsa, laying around Aloysius's estate to recover from travel. Most of the laying around was done in the bedroom or at the lake. Unfortunately, they soon had to leave for one of the last stops on the marriage tour–a city called Victorie. It wasn't as large as Chauvi, which was the largest city in the Westerlands, although it was tiny compared to Raulle. Amaria had been unable to stop herself from comparing her new home to her old. It was unfair, she knew, but it was hard to stop.

But Amaria was excited for Victorie. She visited the city before and loved it. Victorie was on the outskirts of the Westerlands and wasn't even half a day's ride from the Lierre Fideles. A small part of the city even crossed into the Arbres Dorés province, even though Victoria was a Westanni city. And the western side of the drawbridge that led over the lake to get from the western side of the Westerlands to Victorie was so close to Sauvegarde Coroline.

In many ways, Victorie was more a cultural center fitting of a capital than the actual Thestitiunian capitol, Aionstown. The only province without easy access was Perivina Fluere.

The trip from Monsa to Victorie wasn't long, only lasting a two day's ride. Amaria and Theodmon were dropped off right outside the gates of the Chauvignon's summer home, Aurea Nikevia, instead of having to hike through the hills.

The palace was empty with only a few servants managing the place. It was clean, not a speck of dust to be found on any bannister or railing, but the vases were empty and the tables bare.

Amaria wrapped her arms around herself, even though there was no chill. Even for a summer palace, this was a desolate place. Aurea Nikevia wasn't abandoned, but there was no life or joy within its golden halls.

"It used to be more lively," Theodmon said. "My family and I used to vacation here for months every year."

"Used to? Why don't you anymore?"

Theodmon sighed, sitting down on the stone stairs in the middle of the foyer, his hand brushing over the golden griffin engravings on the pillar next to him. "It just didn't feel the same after my father's death. Ophelia and Aloysius never got along well with Mother, and I was so busy stepping into my role as Marquis...." Theodmon trailed off, placing his head in his hands. "It was too painful."

Amaria's heart twisted inside her chest as she reached out towards Theodmon, wrapping her arms around him, embracing him from behind. She had her differences with her siblings and her father, but not so much that the entire family unit collapsed after her mother's death. She couldn't imagine what Theodmon had endured–he was so young when he became Marquis.

"We didn't have to come here. We can turn around, head back to Monsa–"

"I wanted to." Theodmon kissed her hands, not removing himself from her embrace. "It's a beautiful palace and I want to enjoy it again. We can make new memories here."

Amaria pushed her body closer against Theodmon's, laying her head on his shoulders. She could only pray to the gods that all the memories she would build with him would be positive. For all their wealth and security, both of them dealt with too much–the death of a father, the death of a mother, the death of a friend, a fiancé who beat her, the responsibility of an entire duchy on his shoulders, and the grieving of the people they never got to be.

"We will endure," Amaria whispered to herself.

"Hmm?" Theodmon kissed her hands and arms again.

"Nothing," Amaria said. "Just that I am looking forward to our new memories together."

Chapter Fourteen

After a few days in Victoire, Theodmon and Amaria departed, heading towards the westernmost mountain border city, Auberville. "These mountains are the only protection we have from the Nagalia Aride."

The Nagalia Aride was the inhospitable desert that bordered Thestitiunia. Amaria hadn't ever considered it, besides as a passing thought in geography class, because her home was so far away from it. And the Westerlands were filled with lush forests–it seemed almost ridiculous that they needed the mountains to protect them from a dry, dead land.

"There's been a few times where sandstorms have swept over the mountains," Theodmon continued with a chuckle as the carriage rolled to a stop. "The merchants sell Nagalia Aride sand as a novelty when it happens."

"Surely not," Amaria said, although she believed the merchants did sell that and at an exorbitant price, likely with claimed powers and properties that didn't exist.

"Sometimes the sand is white, or yellow, or pink, or black, or blue."

"The many colored sands." Amaria remembered her tutors had once said something about that in a lesson. It felt so long ago.

Theodmon stepped out of the carriage. "I'm sure we can find a bottle for you, if you'd want one."

"What magic properties am I getting?" Amaria teased, her eyes twinkling. laughed, holding out his arm to help her exit the carriage.

"Whatever the merchant thinks he can sell to you."

"You think they'll lie about magic properties to me?" Amaria pointed to her silver eyes. "I'm a rather distinctive individual."

"Yes, you are immediately apparent as a wealthy and powerful mage," Theodmon noted, and Amaria noticed he focused his gaze on not only her eyes but her dress and jewels. "So it'll be a toss up if the merchant thinks he's scamming a rich noble or a mage who will know better."

"Shall we test it?" Amaria asked, the two of them walking through the cobblestone streets.

"You just want to see someone panic." Theodmon shook his head with a smile. "Alright, let's find a merchant for you to terrify."

The two of them walked through the streets of Auberville, stopping in the merchant and artisan district, where townspeople were shouting, peddling their wares.

"Glassware! Best in the city!"

"Herbs, tonics, and potions!"

"Roasted turkey legs!"

"No sand yet," Theodmon muttered under his breath, laughing.

"They have to be somewhere around here." Amaria craned her head to look and see if there was any bottled sand in sight.

For a few more minutes, the two of them wandered through the bustling marketplace, not seeing anyone selling sand.

"Perhaps they're not here today," Theodmon said, sounding disappointed.

"It's alright." Amaria squeezed his arm. "We should get on the road before dark, right?"

"My Lady," a man with a ponytail called out. "Would you like to buy something magical?"

Amaria paused, keeping the hood of her riding cloak up and her back turned the merchant. "Magic?"

"Oh yes," the man said wheezily. "Sand from the Nagalia Aride. It can cure disease. I have a bottle corked by a wind mage."

Amaria turned towards him, lowering the hood of cloak, her silver eyes boring into him. She noticed that he blinked quickly, taking a step back as his gaze averted from meeting her eyes. Behind her, Theodmon coughed, stepping away from the scene.

"What sort of wind mage bothered themselves to collect specks of dirt?" Amaria asked. "That's all sand is, isn't it? Pretty specks of dirt."

"Are you a wind mage? Of course you are, the eyes," the merchant said, his eyes shifting between Amaria and Theodmon. "I meant that earth mages–"

"I'm also an earth mage," Amaria's hand brushed against a small bottle of pink sand. "And there's no magic radiating from any of your wares." She picked up the bottle. "But this is a pretty color, I'll take it."

"Five drag–"

"You misunderstood me," Amaria said. "I am not buying it."

"I'll-"

"Call the guards?" Theodmon scoffed. "Please, continue. I am sure the guards would be eager to help a snake oil salesman arrest Marchioness Chauvignon."

"Marchioness?" The merchant paled as he looked at Theodmon. "Marquis, forgive me, I didn't know–"

"Obviously," Theodmon snapped. "If you're going to scam people, at least be halfway intelligent about it." He looked over towards Amaria, a half smile tugging on his lips. She sighed, forcing back her own smile.

"Let's go," he directed, holding out his arm for her.

"Next time, don't try to scam powerful mages, like Extractors, with faux magical items," Amaria called out over her shoulder as she took Theodmon's arms. "We can sense magic."

And it was common knowledge mages could sense magic. Or so I thought. Amaria looked down at the small bottle of pink sand in her hand. *At least I got this souvenir.*

"You enjoyed that," Theodmon noted as they meandered through the marketplace.

Amaria beamed. "Yes," she admitted. "Is that awful of me?"

Theodmon looked at her, saying nothing for a while. "Some might say that, but no. I don't think you're awful. I think I'm slightly more attracted to you."

And she was more attracted to him as well. Amaria's heart fluttered. "Is there a hunting lodge here?"

"No, but there's an estate about two hours north."

Amaria bit her lip. "And are we going to engage in extracurricular activities in the carriage?"

Theodmon laughed, squeezing her hand as they approached the carriage, Amaria handing over her bottle to a footman to pack in her trunk. "I'm going to make you wait."

"That's cruel," Amaria teased.

"I thought you liked cruelty," Theodmon tsked, holding out his hand and helping her back into the carriage.

Amaria laughed, sitting down in her seat and spreading out her deep blue skirts. "Not against myself."

"It's penance for the torture you put that poor merchant through." Theodmon smirked. "I think you gave him nightmares."

"He made the mistake of attempting to scam an Extractor," Amaria protested, laughing.

"I don't think scamming the Extractor was the mistake," Theodmon said as the carriage began to move, departing from Auberville. "I think him trying to scam a Raulet was his downfall."

"Not a Chauvignon?" Amaria questioned. "These are your lands."

"And Raulets are notoriously wealthy and temperamental," Theodmon said. "When it comes to merchants, you are a monster of a caliber I could never hope to reach."

"A monster?" Amaria's eyebrows rose.

"A compliment," Theodmon assured her. "Being terrifying is a skill you should never be ashamed of."

"I'm not." Amaria leaned back in her seat. "Where are we headed tomorrow? After we've stayed at the estate?"

Theodmon sighed. "We'll be heading back towards Chauvi, likely stopping at a few more estates, villages, and Dovesport beforehand."

"The tour is almost over?" Amaria couldn't hide the disappointment in her voice.

"The only two major cities I've not shown you are Maulleries and Valeville."

"The fortress cities?" Amaria questioned, knowing that Maulleries was the closest city to Percipes Pass and Rindria and that Valeville was the closest city to Morroek, protected only by the soldiers guarding the Valemont Tunnels.

"They're not particularly romantic. I didn't want to ruin the wedding tour with the stench of a soldier who hadn't bathed in half a year."

"Are there no baths at the forts or their cities?"

"Of course there are, they just don't have it as high importance, much to the healing mages despair. The amount of letters I have from the mages stationed there about infection...."

"Does Lord Delaluna not handle the mages?" Amaria questioned.

"He does. But these are more of a soldier's issues, not a mage's, even though the mages wish they could force them to bathe."

"Lord Delaluna could force them," Amaria stated, aware of the complexities of Henri's magic and how he could alter and break people's thoughts, mind, and will. "He might be the most powerful mage in the world."

Theodmon tilted his head wryly at her. "I've heard you're pretty powerful yourself."

"I can make plants grow, summon flames, shoot ice from my hands," Amaria dismissed. "Henri can alter people's memories and thoughts." She wasn't denying she was powerful, but she wasn't going to deny that sometimes she felt dwarfed by Henri's power. She was a liar, but she wasn't foolish enough to be that deluded. She leaned forward, meeting Theodmon's eyes. "I wish this tour wasn't ending so soon. I enjoy spending time with you."

"Only spending time?" Theodmon grasped her hands. "I was going to say I was fond of you, perhaps even growing to love you."

Amaria's mouth turned dry. She wanted to love Theodmon and she wanted him to love her, but it was inconceivable that someone could love her after only a few weeks of knowing her. But he was her husband, she had no escape from him except for death. What was the harm in admitting that she was fond of him as well, and that she too, perhaps, was growing to love him.

Theodmon was kind, intelligent, handsome, and she was beginning to feel as if she could be herself around him–as if he could see her bare and not be terrified and disgusted by what he saw. He called her Aaron Raulet's creature, but it hadn't been judgmental. *It's true. I am his creature.* But that statement didn't matter now. Not when Theodmon had just accepted her, despite her *talents*. And he said she was adept at torture–that he would want to utilize that skill set.

She wouldn't have to give up a part of herself, drowning it until it was beaten down, with him. She could be free without giving up security and safety.

"I'm fond of you too." Amaria leaned forward to where her nose brushed against Theodmon's. "And I want to say I love you, but–"

"It's alright," Theodmon interrupted.

"No." Amaria kissed him on the cheek. "I am growing to love you, and I might already–gods, we are already bound! Why can't I say this?"

"I love you too." Theodmon leaned forward and gave her a peck on the lips. "Now come here and lay in my arms until we arrive at the country estate."

Chapter Fifteen

They departed the next day for Fortresses les Blanche. Amaria found herself resting in the carriage, snacking on jerky, and playing card games with Theodmon as they traveled through the fields and forests of the Westerlands.

And while in part she was anxious to not be trapped in a carriage, she did feel a sadness when they were on the outskirts of Chauvi. She enjoyed the time she spent with her new husband, and in truth, she wasn't ready to depart from the easy comfort they had.

Theodmon had responsibilities he had to attend to and she could predict that her own responsibilities would soon become apparent.

"Amaria," Theodmon said as the carriage climbed up the mountain. "We'll have to get out of the carriage and go up by foot to Forteresse les Blanche. There's a point where it'll be too steep to continue up the mountain with the weight of our luggage."

Amaria nodded, remembering that trek too well. And she remembered the pulley system she saw for supplies but decided to not ask further questions about it. "At least I have boots."

Theodmon laughed. "Is it bad that I was hoping the lack of easy access to my estate would deter certain guests at our wedding?"

"I was hoping so too," Amaria admitted. "But you made adequate accommodations to get even the most elderly noble into the dining hall."

"A horrible decision on my part," Theodmon said dryly. "I wish weddings could be more private."

Amaria could understand the sentiment, and in part she agreed. But her dress had been beautiful and exorbitant and she enjoyed wearing it to flaunt her beauty and wealth. "There's some benefit to the current system."

"Which is?"

"Enemies being forced to wish you well and call you beautiful," Amaria giggled. "I thought Durek Svilas was going to die."

"He conducted himself better than some," Theodmon noted as the carriage came to a stop. "But yes, that was entertaining. Ah, this is our cue." Theodmon stood up, swiftly departing from the carriage, giving Amaria his hand as she climbed out.

Amaria scanned the mountainside, appreciating it at dusk, the birds chirping.

Theodmon trudged up the mountain. "I have a gift for you waiting inside–provided it was completed on time."

He's gotten me so many gifts. "Is it the sheath for my dagger?"

"No," Theodmon said, "although that should be ready as well."

It wasn't necessary for him to shower her with so many gifts. However, Amaria was not going to admit that to him. Instead she bowed her head. "I can't wait to see what you've given me."

They silently completed their trek, stopping only once they were inside the white stone walls of Forteresse les Blanche. Amaria took her traveling cloak off as Theodmon beckoned a page, who was holding a small velvet box, over to them. "I hope you enjoy it, Ammy."

"Ammy?"

"A nickname," Theodmon explained. "If you don't like it-"

"I do," Amaria assured him, surprising herself with the truth of the statement. "I've just not had a nickname before."

"Really?" Theodmon's jaw dropped slightly.

"I suppose that's not technically true." Amaria shook her head. "Haerdnor would call me Am sometimes, in private, and I'd call him Haer—but it was never around others or in public...."

"Why?" Theodmon peered into her eyes. Amaria felt tension leaving her body as she smiled at him, taking in how his eyes seemed as warm as honey. She could have looked into those eyes for a million years.

"My father doesn't like nicknames."

Next to them, the page handed Theodmon the box, inclining his head. Theodmon took the box from him and opened it, revealing a silver necklace of a rose, thorns and all, with leaves made from black pearls. Her heart fluttering, Amaria watched as Theodmon removed the necklace from the box, handing the empty box to the page with a dismissal, before he turned his attention back to her.

"For you," Theodmon gestured for her to turn around, and she obliged. "I tried to make it representative, so I got a rose because it's as beautiful as you." He clasped the necklace shut on her neck, it dangling over her collarbone. "As for the pearl petals, well you're as rare and perfect as they are." Theodmon turned her around and looked at her. She had tears in her eyes, even though she was trying to suppress them.

"They're beautiful," Amaria complimented.

Black pearls couldn't have been easy to find, especially this far inland. Theodmon must have commissioned this the day he asked for her favorite jewels. Her eyes burned, and Amaria blinked to prevent tears from falling.

"Do you like it?"

"I adore it."

"My Lord." A guard approached them and bowed towards Theodmon. "My Lady," he greeted Amaria out of politeness before turning back to Theodmon. "I know you just returned, but we've been unable to locate Lord Bécharil. The person of interest is in the Labyrinths."

Theodmon sighed. "Thank you," he told the guard. "You may go."

As the guard left, Amaria tilted her head, looking at Theodmon. "Person of interest? Do you mean the Mortensia Labyrinths?" Amaria named the Chauvignon's notorious prison, carved from the mountain itself, as casually as listing a wine list.

"I wish Lucas was here, he's better at this sort of thing. I'm sorry, I have to go deal with this."

"I'm assuming 'unable to locate' is code?"

Theodmon nodded. "Likely on another assignment–Lucas does a lot of dirty work—it's unimportant. This is time sensitive."

"What is it?"

Theodmon cast a glance down the hallway as he stepped closer to Amaria, his voice lowered. "There's a suspected spy. He was running information that weakens our border with Rindria."

"Rindria?" Amaria said sharply, remembering the intelligence she had recently gathered from the Drowning Tombs. "Let me question him."

"Are you sure?" Theodmon asked. "We just got home, I know you want to settle in–"

"You told me that you heard I was an adept torturer, right?"

Theodmon looked at her unblinkingly, his hazel eyes a kaleidoscope of emotions Amaria could not decipher. Perhaps he didn't want her to be an unusual bride, perhaps he was bothered by her being Aaron Raulet's creature and he lied to her. Or perhaps he told the truth.

If she could do this, torture a man in front of Theodmon, she would truly know how he felt. And when she had knowledge she could adequately adjust how she acted around him for the rest of her life. She was growing to love him, but how this relationship progressed would be determined not at a ball or the marriage bed, but in the dungeons.

"Of course," Theodmon replied.

"Then let me prove my reputation."

The Griffin and the Rose

Chapter Sixteen

Theodmon led Amaria through the grounds, stopping outside a black stone door carved into the mountain. The guards opened the doors, allowing Theodmon to step inside, but thrust their arms out, blocking Amaria from following.

"Apologies, Marchioness, but this isn't a place for a lady."

Theodmon turned around, intending to say something, however Amaria, her eyes flashing already was glaring at the guards. "What's my name?"

"Marchioness Chauvingon...." the guard said hesitantly.

Amaria cooly surveyed the guard and Theodmon had to stop himself from smiling. "What is my name? The name I was born with."

The guard wet his lips. "Amaria Raulet."

Amaria nodded. "Have you heard any rumors associated with that name and the Drowning Tombs? I'm ordering you to answer honestly."

The guard looked over towards Theodmon, his eyes wide. "I've heard a few things, I'm not sure if there is any credibility to it–"

"I didn't ask your opinion on whether what you heard was credible," Amaria said. Theodmon coughed, hiding his smile into his sleeve as he felt his heart swell. "Tell me what you heard."

The guard swallowed, looking over at Theodmon. Theodmon shook his head, nodding towards this guard, commanding him to answer the question.

The guard looked at his boots, his lips barely moving. "You torture people there."

"That's credible." Amaria stepped closer to the guard. "If I torture people in the Drowning Tombs, what makes the Mortensia Labyrinths different?"

Theodmon bit his lip, stepping forward. "Let her in. Thank you for your diligence. For future reference, you are to give my wife every access in the castle, including these prisons. In that regard, treat her the same as you would treat me. Understand?"

"Yes, my Lord." The guard looked up from his boots, standing at attention.

Theodmon held out his hand to her. She stepped past the guard and slipped her hand into his, squeezing it as they walked down the stairs, the door shutting behind them, darkness encompassing them. Beside him, Theodmon heard Amaria take a sharp breath, pulling her hand out of his.

She's scared of the dark. You idiot, torches should have been li–

A flickering of fire appeared in Amaria's hands, illuminating the space around them. Theodmon turned, looking over at her. Her face was impassive, flickering in the shadows of the flames.

"Where's the prisoner?"

Amaria showed no sign of weakness or apprehension.

"Follow me." Theodmon led her through the prison, stopping only when they reached the cell of Matthieu Touchard. "All we know is he was found entering and exiting the Rindria side multiple times."

"And he's a foot soldier? A courier? Calvary?" Amaria questioned.

"Foot soldier," Theodmon confirmed. Perhaps the other two wouldn't have been as suspicious.

Amaria bit her lip, tilting her head to the side. "Do you know where he's from? Is it somewhere like Dovesport? Victorie? Or a border village?"

"I believe it was Maulleries." A jolt went up his spine. "Why?"

Amaria shook her head, lifting a finger to her lips. She turned to the guard. "Let me in. What tools are in this chamber?"

The guard looked over towards Theodmon, as if seeking guidance on what to do. Theodmon shrugged. Amaria knew what she was doing, and the guards would soon learn that.

The guard turned back towards Amaria. "We have a rack, thumbscrews, rat cages, poisons–"

"Is there an Oxmera's Cradle?"

Theodmon's head whipped over to stare at Amaria. Oxmera's Cradle was a pyramid-shaped seat with a pointed tip in which the victim would be placed with their legs bound as they were lowered onto the sharp point. It made Theodmon squeamish and he had a high tolerance for these sorts of things.

The guard gave a large swallow. "We usually reserve that for the guilty–"

"And who told you he wasn't guilty?" Amaria said. "Keep defending spies and I may begin to question your loyalty."

Theodmon forced back a snort as the guard took a step back. His eyes were glued to Amaria. She was unruffled, collected. She had a plan, and although Theodmon couldn't fathom all the parts of it yet–mainly why she was planning on using Oxmera's Cradle, he respected how she calmly gave commands as if she was born to it.

"Go," she dismissed the guard.

"Are you starting with–"

"I would have told you if I was planning on starting with Oxmera's Cradle. Leave. Don't speak, I don't want to hear it."

Theodmon pinched his nose, looking at his feet as he bit his lower lip. She was terrifying. She was magnificent. The rumors of her were true, Amaria was no stranger to a dungeon. How fascinating it would be to see her in action.

"Why the Cradle?" Theodmon asked as he stepped forward to unlock the cell.

"It's to make an example of him," Amaria said. "Either he is a spy and deserves it, or he's innocent and we've inadvertently made an enemy who will run to Rindria and we risk weakening our border. I'm not taking that risk, he'll die regardless."

It was cruel. It was unfair. Theodmon didn't disagree. He respected her blatant ruthlessness, a trait he rarely saw in highborn ladies. But one thing didn't make sense–how could an example be made if it wasn't public?

The door to the cell was open however, and Theodmon knew better to ask these sorts of things in front of prisoners.

The spy curled in a ball, his ragged clothes torn. "I won't eat." His voice was raspy.

"A hunger strike." Amaria stepped closer to the prisoner. "How quaint that you think that has any impact on your time here."

"You can't poison-"

Amaria grabbed the man's chin, forcing him to look at her. "You don't deserve an easy death. Treason. Espionage. Tell me one good reason I'd let you die in your sleep instead of flaying you and making you watch as I burn your fingers that I chopped off."

The man coughed, looking over towards Theodmon. "A woman won't do these things."

A flame sparked on Amaria's pointer finger, the shadows dancing across her face. A chill went through Theodmon's spine as he saw the smile she had as she placed the flames on the spy's arm, his shouts echoing in the small cell.

"Confess," she whispered. Theodmon's heartbeat quickened. She was beautiful. A figure of merciless death. "I am a woman. Perhaps I can help you." The flames died down. "I am good at this, but I don't prefer it. Let's come to an understanding. Why are you here?"

Theodmon noticed that her eyes were widened, and her face contorted in a believable, but false, empathy. Theodmon's throat bobbed. Had she manipulated him?

The man adjusted himself on the cot. "I have nothing to confess."

"Then tell me why you crossed between Rindria and Thestitiunia." Amaria's voice was soft, barely carrying through the cell.

The man swallowed. "It's a misunderstanding."

Amaria stroked his cheek. "I'm sure."

"If I tell you, am I free to go?"

"If it's an innocent reason, I can assure you that you will be leaving this prison today."

Theodmon's eyebrows rose, and he was thankful the shadows concealed him. Amaria had indicated she was going to kill him and yet she sounded as if she wasn't lying.

The chains rattled as the man wrung his hands together. "There's a Riam girl. I love her."

Amaria sat down next to him on his cot. "Love is wonderful." She grasped his hands in hers, looking the prisoner directly in the eye. "I was recently married. It's like finding parts of myself I didn't even know existed. And to be with my husband for years is a blessing." She sighed, leaning against the wall. "What's her name?"

"Madeline Wheatfield," the prisoner said.

Amaria hugged herself, her eyes turning glassy. "Is she a wheat farmer? Or is her father one?"

The man was silent, the only noise was the breathing of all three people in the cell. "I shouldn't say."

"She was married, wasn't she?" Amaria gave a singular clap as her jaw dropped. "Oh my."

The man spat at Amaria. "War time is hard!"

Theodmon snorted, realizing too late how this man had to meet Madeline. She was selling herself over the border, trying to earn coins for her family. The man glared at him.

"Ignore my husband," Amaria soothed. "He doesn't understand these things. I do." Amaria kindly looked at the prisoner. "Did she know that you weren't–"

"She knew I was Thestitiunian."

Amaria stood up, grinning. "I love a forbidden love story. Especially when it's between two spies." She turned towards the exit, motioning for Theodmon to follow her. "Madeline is one of mine."

Theodmon took a step back, blinking. "You...you weren't searching for information." She had been searching for confirmation.

Amaria's face flushed as she looked at her feet as they stepped out of the cell, the wooden door thudding behind them. "I hope this doesn't change your opinion of me."

"Have you lied to me?"

Amaria's eyes widened. "No." Her voice cracked. "Never."

Theodmon gripped her shoulders. "I'll make you a promise, but I need one in return. We will never lie to each other."

Amaria gulped, giving him a small nod, tears welling in her eyes. "I never will. I promised you that. I want us to have a good relationship. How I act with prisoners isn't how I'd act with my family–you can ask my father, my siblings–"

Theodmon pulled her into a hug, a pang in his chest. "I know," he whispered. "I trust you." He had only needed the confirmation. She was so unlike anyone he had met before, it was sometimes difficult to determine how he should ask.

"You were brilliant in there. But I must ask, where is Oxmera's Cradle coming into play? Are you still using it?"

Amaria's eyes shone as she held his hands, squeezing them as she beamed. "Plant a spy who confesses," Amaria whispered to Theodmon. "Within the week. Chain all the suspected spies together in the cell with Oxmera's Cradle. Have this scum be executed in front of them, and make it an event of releasing the one who 'confessed.'"

Theodmon pulled her into a kiss, his lips locking with hers as he pulled her head closer to him. He knew that this wouldn't make most of the spies confess and give information, but if it incentivized even one, they could have invaluable information.

It was a convoluted, yet ingenious plan. Amaria was brilliant, extraordinary even, and she was all him. Theodmon wanted to fuck her right now. But she wouldn't like to be fucked on a dungeon floor, and besides, the blood was un-sanitary.

He needed to have her now and couldn't restrain for much longer. "Let's get to our chambers." He kissed her.

Amaria tilted her head back, breathing through her nose. "Chambers," she whispered. "Quickly."

Amaria laid on Theodmon's chest, her fingers twirling his chest hair as their naked, sweaty bodies entwined with each other. As soon as they returned from the Mortensia Labyrinths, they fucked for nearly an hour.

Theodmon needed Amaria, she was intoxicating. From the smell of her perfume, to the softness of her skin, and the intelligence she had, as well as that determination–she could accomplish moving mountains if she wanted to.

And she was as depraved as him, if not more. He didn't have to hide himself from her. And despite her showcasing her ability to lie as easily as she breathed, Theodmon trusted her. He knew that he shouldn't. Aloysius called her a beautiful snake for a reason. But she had been so open with him about her friend's death. Amaria had been so vulnerable with him on their wedding night.

Perhaps it was a ruse, but Theodmon didn't believe it was. Amaria had an incentive for him to trust her and she seemed to want a genuine connection with him. And he wanted one with her. He didn't want to hide himself with her–he wanted her to be the one person who saw every aspect of himself. Everyone else knew a small facet of his personality, a façade based on what part they expected to see.

He didn't want to hide from at least one person. Sighing, he looked over to see the half-finished tapestry Amaria had been crafting. There were roses, griffins, money, and a sword with a man and a woman embracing in the center.

He was beginning to love her. Theodmon wanted to be with her almost every waking moment. There was a hunt coming up, and while he enjoyed hunts normally, he was dreading this one. Being away from Amaria for days would feel like torture.

"Come with me."

Amaria laid her head on his chest, smiling. "Hmm?"

"I have a hunt coming up. Come with me."

Amaria tilted her eyes upwards. "I'm an awful rider–"

"I'll help you." Theodmon pulled Amaria tighter against him. "Come with me."

Amaria sighed. "Alright."

Theodmon stroked her hair, marveling at how soft it was. He loved her. She was beautiful, intelligent, and haunted. He was haunted and like moths to a flame, he was drawn to her for that. Both of them had both been through so much and Theodmon realized that they both needed the same thing.

"I want revenge on Rindria." Theodmon's confession rang in the silence that followed. "You do too. I promise you, we will get it. And once we get it, we will heal our grief."

Amaria sat up, leaning forward as she looked at Theodmon, her silver eyes unblinking. "How can you promise that?"

Theodmon sat up, meeting her eyes. It was a fair question, and without answering it he would be giving a promise that was a delusion of grandeur. He wet his lips, trying to vocalize how he felt, how he knew that the downfall of those who hurt them would patch the grief they both felt. It was an impossible task.

Moments passed, an owl hooting outside. Theodmon stood up to pour himself wine from the pitcher. Amaria followed him. And as he handed her a goblet, the words struck him as if they were lightning.

"Revenge grants closure."

Chapter Seventeen

"You've never been on a hunt before," Nicoletta told Amaria as a maid pinned Amaria's hat onto her hair. "Why now? You never showed an interest."

"I was never allowed to show an interest," Amaria corrected cooly.

"You think your father would have an issue with you killing animals?" Nicoletta snorted, crossing her arms.

"Who said that was what he disapproved of?" Amaria raised an eyebrow. "There's more issue with hunting than the violence."

"Oh?" Nicoletta challenged.

"Hunting is a activity that men do and riding a horse could damage-look, Duke Vypren was traditional and we didn't want any wayward accusations of-"

"Okay," Nicoletta interrupted. "I get it."

Amaria scowled. "Glad I had to spell it out for you." Delphina wouldn't have needed this explained—she would have just understood. Amaria cast a small glance over at Nicoletta, feeling a sudden twinge of guilt. "That was mean."

"Yes," Nicoletta agreed.

"I'm an awful rider," Amaria admitted. "And I'm worried about that."

The maid stepped back giving a small curtsy. Amaria waved her hand dismissing her.

"I'm sure Marquis Chauvignon won't hold that against you," Nicoletta said.

"I agree," Amaria said. But that didn't mean she wanted to ruin the hunt with her incompetence. "I'm still worried." She stood up, brushing down the folds of her dark green dress. "Let's get breakfast." She held out her hand towards Nicoletta as if it were an olive branch. "I know you enjoy the cherry pastries."

Nicoletta gave a soft chuckle, ducking her head as she took Amaria's hand. She smiled, and allowed Amaria to lead her from the chambers and through the corridors to the great hall.

Once they reached the great hall, the two of them sat on a bench nearest to the exit, eating their food.

"Ammy," a male voice said behind her, as she felt a hand on her shoulder. Amaria's head whipped around, looking upwards at her husband.

"Theo!" she greeted with a beam.

"Theo?" He chuckled. "Did Aloysius tell you that?"

Amaria rolled her eyes. "It's the most obvious nickname for you. I figured I should give you one too."

Theodmon gave a short laugh. "Fair enough. Are you ready to depart? I have a crossbow ready for you."

"Thank you but that's unnecessary." Amaria stood up from the bench and next to Theodmon. "I prefer my magic as a weapon, I am much more adept there."

"Mages," Theodmon muttered, shaking his head. "I'll never understand." He smiled good-naturedly at her. "But you're ready to leave?"

Amaria nodded. "Of course." She looked over at Nicoletta and bid her goodbye as she departed with Theodmon, reaching the group milling around the entryway to the castle foyer. As they approached, Juliette and another woman, bulky in size, approached her.

"Juliette," Amaria greeted. "And you are?" she asked the other woman.

"Lady Brigitte Belamy, Marchioness," she said.

"I'm so glad you're coming with us." Juliette grabbed Amaria's hands. "We need more women on hunts."

"You go on hunts?" Amaria noticed that Juliette did not have a weapon on her. This was unlike Brigitte, who had a sword and a crossbow.

Juliette laughed. "The rabbits don't know what's coming. I use my magic to hunt–it's similar to yours but I am only Hydra Blessed, not Dragon Blessed as well."

Amaria laughed. "Earth and Water."

"Ice spikes and mud pits," Juliette agreed. "It's delightful. We're going to have so much fun."

Amaria rolled her neck as the horses trotted to a stop near the lake. Lake Holimeda was vaster than Amaria expected. She knew it bordered Chauvi and Dovesport but now, as they ventured west deep into the woods. However, she hadn't expected that she wouldn't be able to see any sort of civilization as the horses drank.

Theodmon's horse trotted next to hers. "How are you enjoying it?"

"It's more riding, less killing than I expected." Amaria's pelvis hurt, and she was an awful rider. She knew she was holding everyone back, and she despised herself for it.

Theodmon chuckled. "Sometimes that happens."

"Are you hoping for a specific animal?" Amaria asked. "A bear or deer or boar?"

"A boar would be fun," Theodmon agreed. "But nothing in particular. I'd not object to a unicorn however."

"A unicorn?" Most people tried to avoid the blood-thirsty beasts, especially non-mages as unicorns tended to lure in people with their magic. Mages weren't immune, but there tended to be enough pushback from their magic for them to escape before they lost their wits.

Theodmon pulled out a large ruby necklace from under his shirt. "I have protection." Amaria peered at the gem. She could see the remnants of magic within the gem pounding against its captivity.

"When's the last time you refilled this?" Her hands reached out for the necklace.

Theodmon's eyebrows scrunched together as her hands circled around the gem. "Why?"

She closed her eyes, breathing steadily as she summoned a stream of her magical energy, forcing it into the gem. "You were running low on magic." She opened her eyes to look directly into Theodmon's. "This would have protected you against one, maybe two unicorns, but any more than that you would have willingly walked into their lair and died."

His eyes widened. "Thank you."

"I'd hate to become a widow."

Theodmon laughed. "I'll try to avoid that." He pulled out his sword, inspecting the blade in the sunlight. He sheathed his sword and pulled the crossbow from his back. "I think the horses are done resting, let's go find something to hunt, shall we?"

As the group rode deeper into the forest, Amaria looked upwards. Despite it being midday, the daylight disappeared into dusk. The canopy was claimed by sycamore, asp, and elm, and curling tree limbs suspended all around them. Around them, a flower, appearing to be made from white and silver glass, sparkled and reflected in the sunlight.

Amaria's hand reached out to touch the white and silver flower almost as if she was in a trance. "That's Myphy's Jewel. If you use it in your earth magic, it can apparently make you incredibly powerful...."

Amaria wanted to gather every single flower there. There was something dangerous about Myphy's Jewel–it was named in connection with the god of vengeance, but truly, who cared? Amaria couldn't remember the danger and if she couldn't remember, it couldn't have been that important, could it?

"There's also belladonna," Lucas accounted for the deadly herb as he pulled his horse to a stop. "Give me a moment," he directed, before dismounting and gathering the plants.

"Lucas!" Juliette protested.

Lucas shrugged. "My poison stock was running low. Freshly picked is better than anything I'd buy from a merchant."

Theodmon unsheathed his sword, his eyes darting around the forest. "Myphy's Jewel should not be here."

Amaria knew he was right. There was something wrong, but the call of power was ringing in her ears. Lucas was gathering his plants. Why couldn't she gather hers? Perhaps Juliette would also like to help. She was an earth mage too. Perhaps she could use the newfound power to destroy everyone in her path as she avenged Delphina's death. She wanted the world to burn.

Delphina should have never died. Amaria couldn't bring her from the Silent Kingdom but she could send others there. Delphina didn't deserve to die, the least Amaria could do was punish those who did.

Electricity coursed through Amaria's body. "Something's wrong," she said, her voice barely a whisper. "Something is magically...our magic is being interfered with."

"It's unicorns," Aloysius said. "Gods, did any of you pay attention in lessons?"

Amaria blinked. Unicorns were unnatural, the children of Ghagyn, the goddess of magic and Myphy, the god of vengeance. She supposed she tried to forget about that story because Myphy was also Ghagyn's son–born to her from her husband Vathar, the god of war, strategy, and battle vengeance. Amaria gagged, the intrusive thought of her having a child with her father worming into her mind.

But it was enough to break the spell. She had never fallen under a magical spell like this before–perhaps she was more vulnerable to the god of vengeance's power in the wake of Delphina.

She resisted cursing. She *knew* the signs of a unicorns' spell and yet she still fell under it. She even went as far as warning Theodmon about it.

"Thanks," she told Aloysius.

"You had to say you wanted to hunt a unicorn." Lucas sprinted back to his horse, carrying a bundle of herbs. "Let's get away from here."

"Why?" Theodmon asked. "We have three mages, and me and you have gems. Imagine mounting a unicorn head in your chambers as a trophy."

"Too late," Juliette said, her eyes not drifting away from the pure white animal stepping into the clearing.

The hairs on Amaria's neck stood up as she caught sight of the white horse that stepped into the clearing. It was an unearthly, heavenly white; so pure that the fur upon it seemed to glow. And its mouth was covered in blood.

I need to trap it. Amaria's eyes narrowed as she surveyed the branches and rocks on the forest floor. *If it can't run, we can kill it.* She swung herself off the horse, falling onto her side. She was useless riding, but was secure in using her magic.

Amaria picked herself off the ground, brushing the dirt off her dress. Behind her, Theodmon dismounted. Amaria's eyes did not break from the unicorn. "If Juliette and I trapped it in vines, how fast could you kill it?"

Theodmon loaded his crossbow. "Probably faster than if you didn't-"

Juliette smoothly dismounted, moving towards Amaria. "A wall of earth! Like a stable and they can corner it."

Amaria's mouth dropped open and then turned into a smile. It was brilliant. "Of course!" She turned towards Juliette, her silver eyes sparkling. "I take left and you take right?"

"Add in the back wall for me and a barrier in front for you?" Juliette tossed her braid over her shoulder. "On three?"

Amaria nodded, raising her hands and summoning her magic as she focused on the ground around the unicorn. Behind her, she heard the metallic screech of swords being pulled from their scabbards.

Juliette counted to three, and once the final number was said, Amaria and Juilette raised the walls and Theodmon, Aloysius, and Lucas charged.

The three men slashed at the beast. The unicorn stood on its hind legs, attempting to crush them under its hooves. Mud rose around the unicorn, trapping it and when it lowered its front hooves its body became fully emerged. Only its head and part of its chest was visible.

The unicorn squealed, throwing its head forward as Aloysius jumped to the side to avoid being skewered. As the unicorn threw its head back again, preparing for a second strike, Lucas drove his sword through the unicorn's heart.

The forest was eerily quiet for a few moments. Amaria looked over at Juliette and when she met her brown eyes, Amaria nodded. Together the two girls lowered the walls and the unicorn fell to the ground with a thud.

"So, there's three worthwhile parts. We can have the head mounted, someone can get the hooves, and bones, and the other can have the pelt," Theodmon said.

"The hooves and bones are for poison, so it should be Lucas or you," Aloysius told Theodmon.

"I don't use poison," Theodmon said.

"Your wife does," Aloysius dismissed. "I've heard about her escapades in the Mortensia Labyrinths. So I can either get the pelt or head."

Lucas nodded his head. "Fair. Perhaps we should see if our wives have preferences? After all, they helped kill it."

Juliette rushed towards her husband. "I'd love unicorn furs to wear."

Theodmon looked over at Amaria. "Are you alright with the hooves and bones?"

Amaria stepped closer to him, embracing him. "I've been wanting to experiment with poisons."

Theodmon sighed. "Alright. I get the hooves and bones, Aloysius gets the head, and Lucas gets the pelt. But we're changing it next time we kill one, got it?"

Lucas chuckled as he moved towards the dead unicorn. "How many unicorns do you think we'll be coming across?"

"At least two more," Aloysius grumbled. "Idiot wants a head and a pelt."

Amaria squeezed Theodmon's hand, kissing him on the cheek as the others laughed. Theodmon wanted more despite doing what most people hadn't, and would never do. He killed a unicorn and now he wanted more. That wasn't idiocy, that was ambition.

And Amaria was more attracted to him for it.

Chapter Eighteen

Weeks passed after they had killed a unicorn and Theodmon realized that he had adjusted his habits to form a new schedule compatible with his marriage. He continued to train, however, after training he would now bathe and play card games with Amaria before bed. Along with other things.

Now, he sat on the ground as he watched Lucas and Aloysius wrestle in the middle of the training ring, sweat pouring down their faces as dusk began to fall.

As Theodmon rubbed his sore muscles, Henri sat next to him with a groan. "Five gold dragons on Lucas."

Theodmon chuckled, watching Aloysius grab Lucas squarely around his chest, throwing him to the ground. "I'll take that bet."

Henri leaned forward, his eyes darting between the two competitors. "Lucas can make a comeback."

As Henri spoke, Lucas rolled away from Aloysius, swinging his leg to connect with Aloysius's shins before grabbing him by the legs and bringing him down to the ground.

"Come on Aloysius," Theodmon muttered under his breath. Beside him, Henri was doing similar for his champion.

Aloysius rolled over, somehow placing himself on top of Lucas. The two tousled for a few seconds before Aloysius pinned Lucas down. "One, two, three, four, five," Theodmon counted as Lucas struggled to free himself from Aloysius's grasp. All Aloysius had to do was pin Lucas for ten seconds and Theodmon would be five dragons richer.

Lucas hand tapped the mat three times. Aloysius stood up, holding his hand out towards Lucas. Panting, Lucas accepted Aloysius's hand, and Aloysius pulled his competitor from the ground, helping him to his feet. Both of them clapped each other on the back as they made their way over to Henri and Theodmon.

Theodmon held out his open palm towards Henri. "Hand it over."

Scowling, Henri pulled out his money bag and placed five golden coins in Theodmon's hand.

Aloysius plopped down next to Theodmon. "What's this?"

"I bet on you."

Aloysius brought his hands to his heart. "How touching."

Theodmon rolled his eyes. "It was a good fight."

"Are you feeling well?" Aloysius brought his hand toward Theodmon's forehead.

Theodmon swatted his hand away, scowling. "This is why I don't give you compliments."

"Can we take a walk?" Aloysius's body was still flushed from his fight.

"Rest," Theodmon dismissed.

Henri looked between the two brothers, his eyes widening. "I'm going to bring Lucas to a healing mage—"

Lucas scowled as Henri stood. "I'm fine—"

"I can hear your thoughts rattling," Henri pulled Lucas up to his feet, his knuckles whitening as he gripped Lucas's arm. "You might have a concussion." He whispered something into Lucas's ear.

Lucas stiffened. "Ah yes, I might have a concussion."

Theodmon crossed his arms as he turned towards his brother as the others left. "What were you thinking?"

Aloysius's eyes widened as he brought a hand to his chest. "Me? Why would you think I was thinking anything?"

"You having a brain is a shocking development. But Henri was acting weird in getting us alone. What is it?"

Aloysius shifted his weight from one foot to the other, his shoulders hunched. Theodmon crossed his arms, tapping his foot. Aloysius cleared his throat, but still didn't speak.

"Spit it out."

"So that hunt was something," Aloysius's voice was strained.

Theodmon's eyebrows rose. All of these dramatics over a hunt? "Which one?"

Aloysius rubbed his wrist. "The one with Juliette and Amaria."

Weeks had passed since that hunt. Theodmon's eyes narrowed. "Spit it out."

"I heard about you going to Mortensia Labyrinths with her before that–"

Theodmon stood up. "And?"

"Please," Aloysius stood up, grabbing Theodmon's wrist. "Just listen."

"Two minutes."

"You're defensive of Amaria Raulet," Aloysius commented.

"Chauvignon," Theodmon corrected. "And I have to be, when my own brother is hostile and expects the worst from her."

Aloysius held out his arms, exposing his chest to appear non-threatening. "In my defense, she's a Raulet. It is generally wise to be cautious around them." He took a deep breath. "Do you trust her?"

Theodmon sighed. Aloysius was asking tough questions. But Theodmon couldn't fault him, not for this. He questioned if he trusted Amaria himself after seeing her performance in Mortensia Labyrinths. But he determined that he trusted her because he loved her and that she seemed to love him.

"I trust her. She's self-interested with an uncanny sense of self-preservation–and our interests are aligned."

"And what about when they aren't?"

"She loves me, I think," Theodmon said. "She's loyal. As long as we maintain that relationship she won't turn on me."

"Do you love her?"

"Yes." Theodmon's head fell forward and his stoic demeanor cracking for a moment. "Certain qualities we both have just *merge* together. Yes, there are challenging parts, but I try to be gentle with her. I care for her, and it's not because I have to as her husband. Did you need anything else?" Theodmon's face turned to stone again, smashing his vulnerabilities beneath a mask.

"I'm glad you like your wife." Aloysius stepped away from Theodmon. "I would hate to see history repeat itself."

Theodmon gave a short laugh that sounded more like a bark. The best day of his mother's life had been when his father died. "I'm not looking to suffer."

"They made everyone as miserable as themselves. I just don't want you to end up being the same."

Theodmon closed and opened his fists, breathing through his nose. "I'm trying to avoid that." Contrary to Aloysius's apparent belief, Theodmon wasn't trying to be dismal. It was just that sometimes, being happy was more difficult than succumbing to his own misery. But Amaria changed that, and he hoped it was a permanent change.

Chapter Nineteen

Amaria knotted the end of her embroidery floss, looking at her handiwork. The Union Tapestry was almost done. Aside from the golden rose border, she had added swords, forests, griffins, and a man and a woman embracing in the center. She was working on the waves of the ocean that lapped against the mountains of the forest. The ocean required a multitude of blues, grays, and whites–Amaria sat on the ground, separating the colors she needed. Despite only being back at Forteresse les Blanche for a few weeks, she had made significant progress on this project.

Juliette looked over Amaria's shoulder. "It's coming together."

Amaria picked up a light blue thread. "I hope to be done this week."

She was going to finish the Union Tapestry in under four months of marriage and she had been on her marriage tour for a substantial portion of that. She looked down at her hands, calluses appearing on the tips of her fingers. It was an ambitious goal, but she was going to succeed at it.

"How are other unions going?" Juliette asked.

"What do you mean?" Amaria absentmindedly pulled her thread through the tapestry.

"Are you pregnant?"

Amaria dropped her needle.

"Lady Bécharil!" Nicoletta scolded.

Juliette met Amaria's eyes defiantly. "We're all interested in an heir here. Forgive the intrusion but Chauvignon men have a high risk of death and we've seen so much war–the last thing the Westerlands needs is a succession crisis."

Nicoletta placed her sewing down. "It's been four months–"

"Nicoletta," Amaria warned, not wanting to have to mediate a potential spat. How Juliette asked was blunt, however, Amaria couldn't fault the question. She understood the fears of a succession crisis and knew that her role in this court was not only to bring an infusion of wealth but to ensure that a succession crisis was avoided with heirs and spares.

Juliette looked at Nicoletta. "What do you think the true point of the marriage tour is? Surely you don't think it's to show us around, get us out of a castle?"

Amaria stood up, sensing danger.

Juliette shook her head. "The marriage tour is to have us with our husband, and *only* our husband for weeks. Forgive the crudeness, but how often were you fucked in the carriage?"

Amaria's face flushed. "None of your business."

In truth, she had done it with Theodmon twice, sometimes three times a day. And she didn't dislike the marriage tour.

Juliette held up her hands. "Forgive me."

"I won't," Amaria said.

"I'll say one more thing," Juliette continued. "Our husbands are young and handsome. Respectfully, would you enjoy that tradition with someone other than Marquis Chauvignon?"

"She's only been married for three months," Nicoletta protested, stepping closer to Amaria. "And she asked you to stop, Lady Bécharil."

"Three months is enough." Juliette rubbed her bulging belly. "I'm on my second child and I've been married for two years."

Amaria sat down, trying to remember when she had last bled. Was it during the marriage tour? She hadn't needed rags since she'd returned to Forteresse les Blanche had she? "Juliette," Amaria said hesitantly. "Could you find Katerina Montersat?"

Juliette looked at Amaria, her eyebrow raising before she smiled. "You've not bleed in a while, have you?"

Amaria's heart thudded as she nodded. Juliette beamed, grabbing Amaria's hands. "I'll be back." Juliette almost ran from the room, the door shutting with a thud, leaving behind Nicoletta and Amaria.

Amaria turned towards her friend. "Thank you for your support, but it's unneeded."

"Pregnancy is hard." Nicoletta crossed her arms over her chest. "And you just suffered...Delphina was just murdered in front of us! Do you think adding pregnancy is wise?"

"It doesn't matter," Amaria said. "I'm the eldest daughter of one of the most prominent families in Cesmassia. I was always going to be married to the eldest son of another prominent family and I knew that I was always going to be pregnant as quickly and as often as possible." She looked kindly at Nicoletta. "I have to ensure that the government runs smoothly. What do my feelings matter when compared to preventing thousands of deaths in a civil war?"

"And you would have this stoicism with Vypren?" Nicoletta asked. "Or only Theodmon?"

"The only difference between Vypren and Theodmon is that I am not planning Theodmon's murder. I'd have born Vypren as many children as he demanded, and would mold my sons into who I wanted them to be. Vypren was old–it would not be surprising if he died of an ailment and his five year old son was now the duke."

Nicoletta blinked, taking a small step backwards. "And Theodmon?"

"May the gods let him live a long and happy life," Amaria said. "He's kind, and I care for him." Her hands moved to her stomach, imagining it bulging as she carried Theodmon's child in her womb. She smiled softly, hoping that she was pregnant. Theodmon needed good news, and she was looking forward to carrying his children.

There would be parties in celebration of the pregnancy and eventually, the birth. And Theodmon would give her gifts, praise, and adoration as she carried his child, and even more so if the baby was a boy.

"I love him," Amaria sighed. "I know it seems soon to say, but I do."

"He's a cunning and cruel military leader," Nicoletta hissed. "He killed hundreds with his own hand at Harréow Field. You trust that?"

Amaria's eyes blazed as she scowled at Nicoletta. "I am also cruel and cunning if we are going by reputation. He hasn't hurt me."

"He will," Nicoletta warned. "As soon as he sees past this façade—"

"I've tortured and killed a man in front of him. And he bought me jewelry and fed me cake as he fucked me. We went on a hunt and killed a unicorn together. And through all that he has been gentle with me."

Nicoletta's jaw dropped. "You've been busy."

"I have a reputation," Amaria said chillingly. "And Theodmon was aware of it when he brokered a deal with my father. Who is to say that it wasn't a consideration in his proposal as I am sure my dowry was?"

Nicoletta reached out for Amaria then stopped herself. "Being a Raulet is a powerful weapon, but weapons can be used against their wielders. Be careful."

Amaria looked coldly at Nicoletta. "Please leave. See if you can find my husband and tell him I request his presence in my offices."

"You're summoning him now?" Nicoletta scoffed.

"I'm sure the Court will forgive me if I'm pregnant."

"And if you're not?" Nicoletta challenged. "You'll lose your submissive façade for what gain?"

"Who said I'd lose it?" Amaria challenged. "I was so overjoyed with the thought of being able to tell my husband I was carrying his heir. And when I learned I was not pregnant, I became distraught. In fact I was so distraught that I immediately opened my legs for his pleasure to remedy the situation." Amaria turned away from Nicoletta. "This conversation is over. Leave."

Nicoletta looked at Amaria with drooping eyes but gave a short curtsy before departing.

Amaria sat on her bed, hugging her knees to her chest. Perhaps she shouldn't have been cross with Nicoletta. After all, her childhood friend hadn't meant any harm. And this had to be overwhelming to Nicoletta with her upcoming marriage as well, and her fiance was old. Nicoletta was likely dreading being alone with her husband for weeks–Amaria dreaded the marriage tour when she believed it was with Vypren.

Amaria sighed, picking up her embroidery once more. She might as well be productive while she waited for the healing mage.

After a while, once Amaria embroidered a singular wave, Katerina Montersat came in with a few stalks of barley, setting it in the middle of the floor on top of a tarp. Sighing, Amaria hiked up her skirts, standing over it, forcing herself to think of rainstorms, oceans, and waterfalls until a small trickle poured onto the barley.

"If it sprouts within the next two days, you're pregnant," Katerina said. "Now, let me get some vitals for you. When did you last bleed?" She pressed her fingers against Amaria's neck, feeling a pulse.

"Right before I left for the marriage tour."

"No morning sickness?"

Amaria shook her head.

"If you're pregnant you're likely only around ten weeks," Katerina said. "Thank you, Marchioness. I will let you know the results soon."

As she departed, Theodmon entered the offices. "What's wrong?" He sat beside Amaria.

Amaria smiled sweetly, rubbing his arm, her slender fingers stretching out over his muscles as if they were dancing. "We may have good news in a few days." She rubbed her stomach as she met Theodmon's eyes.

Theodmon sprung up, beaming as he pulled Amaria to her feet and into a hug. "You're pregnant?"

Amaria smiled, tears welling in her eyes as Theodmon picked her up and spun her around, moving closer to the open windows where sunlight was pouring into the rooms. "I hope so, but it's not confirmed."

"We'll have to have parties and feasts to celebrate." Theodmon pulled her into a kiss. "My first child."

Parties were for heirs. Boys. Haerdnor had been celebrated, but even though they were twins, her birth was a passing remark.

"You won't wait until birth? To ensure it's a boy?"

"Why would I? This baby will be my child even if it's a girl, and it's not like I can't afford the celebration. And you'll provide heirs, if not with this child then in time."

The tears in Amaria's eyes intensified as she kissed Theodmon. And as he lifted her skirts and pushed her against the wall, the sunlight bounced off the tears in her silver eyes, turning them into a kaleidoscope of glass.

Chapter Twenty

Theodmon's sword slashed through the practice dummy as the sun rose over the mountains. Despite training for an hour already, Theodmon had been unable to focus. He was making stupid mistakes. He hadn't used a practice dummy since he broke his arm three years ago and was recovering from his injury.

But today was the day the results from Katerina's test were anticipated to be ready. It was best not to spar.

Still, Theodmon didn't know why he was so high-strung. If Amaria was pregnant, she was pregnant, and if she wasn't, they'd try again until she was. He sheathed his sword, determining that he should bathe and prepare himself as best he could for the day. There was nothing he could do, he might as well enjoy whatever happened next.

He wandered through the castle, wandering to one of the more public bathing houses, determining he'd do his best to not wake Amaria. There were a few guards milling around, and they cast him odd glances, but nobody said anything to him as he scrubbed himself down.

After bathing, he went to the gardens and picked a few flowers for Amaria, then made his way up to his chambers, the sun fully up and beaming over the castle.

Once Theodmon entered his chambers, he saw that Amaria was already dressed and sitting at the table, a servant beside her as they set up breakfast. He dismissed the maid as he approached the table.

Amaria turned to face him. The sunlight, pouring in from the windows, bounced off the small golden plate sitting upon her chest, the griffin illuminated.

He kissed her on the forehead. "How'd you sleep?"

Amaria's face paled, her hands running over the rose stitching in her dress. "I had a nightmare."

Theodmon sat next to her at the small circular table. "About what?"

Amaria gulped, shutting her eyes. "I keep seeing Delphina die. The knife that killed her, it was meant for me. *It was meant for me.* It was sent by Clarissa Nalaeny—the Raulet Ruby was stolen, and everything was my fault."

Theodmon placed his hands over hers. "We know where the Raulet Ruby is, right?"

Amaria nodded, tears welling in her eyes.

He kissed her forehead again as a knock pounded on the door. "And the people who have it don't know we know?"

Amaria shook her head. "It's hard to say for sure, but my sources say—"

The door opened, Katerina walking in with a skip in her step as she beamed. "Marquis Chauvignon, Marchioness."

Theodmon looked between her and Amaria. "Is she?"

Katerina nodded. "Yes, my Lord."

Theodmon pulled Amaria into a hug as she smiled. "We'll have to announce it. How many weeks? Do you have a prediction?"

"I believe she is around ten weeks, Marquis. I believe it best if we didn't announce for another three weeks, we want to ensure she safely makes it into the second trimester."

Theodmon nodded absentmindedly, placing his hand over Amaria's stomach. "Of course, whatever you suggest. It'll give me more time to plan the announcement."

"Is there anything else you need?" Katerina asked.

Theodmon looked at Amaria, meeting her eyes in question. She shook her head, smiling.

"You may leave," Theodmon told Katerina. "Thank you."

She gave a small curtsy and departed, leaving Theodmon alone with Amaria.

"I'm amazed I've not been sick yet." Amaria rubbed a hand over her belly. "I've heard the nausea can be almost debilitating." She looked over at her eggs. "Let's eat. We can talk later, I'm starving."

Theodmon chuckled. "I suppose you're eating for two."

Amaria laughed, taking a small bite of her eggs. She gagged, and she stood up, rushing towards the bathing room, and fell to her knees outside the door. She hurled, and vomit erupted over the red carpet.

Theodmon grabbed some bacon and pastries, wrapping them in napkins. "Let's go to the gardens. It's a beautiful day." *And it is easier to clean up vomit from grass than marble and carpet.*

Amaria sniffed, wiping her eyes as she shakily stood.

Theodmon waited for her to approach him, not wanting to get himself or the food too close to the vomit.

"Let's take these next few months to plan our next steps," he said as she neared him. "We'll keep you safe, let us enjoy your pregnancy. And once the baby is born we will be prepared to strike."

Amaria coughed, wiping her mouth. "You'd help me strike at a Riam Princess?"

"Fuck Rindria," Theodmon said. "And yes. I've wanted Rindria to suffer for a while, and I have more reason than ever now. They hurt you." He took a deep breath as they stepped outside his chambers. "They hurt me. I have nightmares too."

"Of what?" Amaria asked, her voice soft.

"I see my father dying. I see the men who died in battle turn into undead." His face burned and he wished he never admitted it, it felt melodramatic in the daylight. However, he was also glad he unburdened himself, that Amaria knew his secret.

She squeezed his hand. "We'll make them pay."

We have a whole year to scheme for it. Theodmon squeezed her hand back. She was amazing, more than he hoped for in a wife. And he believed that as they made plans together she would continue to amaze him. "I am ready to spend forever with you."

Amaria raised herself to give him a peck on the cheek. "And I am ready to scheme."

Juliette Bécharil (Juliette Beh-char-ill): She is originally from Minelle, Avondra. She married Lucas Bécharil and is lady-in-waiting and friend to Amaria Raulet. She is a water and earth mage, commonly called "Hydra Blessed."

Lucas Bécharil (Lucas Beh-char-ill): Currently an untitled Lord. Will be a Marquis once his father dies. He is one of Theodmon Chauvignon's closest friends and bannermen. He is talented with a sword, torture, and tracking.

Ophelia Belegines (Oh-feel-ee-ah Bel-lee-ginny): Mentioned. Previously Ophelia Chauvignon. Eldest daughter of Agatha and Raphael Chauvignon. She is married to Duke Lancelin Belegines of Skeletosa, Avondra.

Mylisana Caeltra (My-les-anna Say-el-traa): Mentioned. A Tressi noblewoman eligible for marriage.

Agatha Chauvignon (Agatha Chauv-ing-non): Widow of Marquis Raphael Chauvignon. Mother of Aloysius, Celestine, Ophelia, and Theodmon. She is from Morroek, and she hates magic and Thestitiunia to a degree.

Aloysius Chauvignon (A-lee-soy-us Chauv-ing-non): Deceased. Youngest son of Agatha and Raphael Chauvignon. A war mage who can harden his body into a shield.

Celestine Chauvignon (Sell-est-tine Chauv-ing-non): Youngest daughter and child of Agatha and Raphael Chauvignon.

Raphael Chauvignon (Raph-ee-elle Chauv-ing-non): Mentioned. Deceased. Father of Theodmon and his siblings. Husband to Agatha Chauvignon.

Theodmon Chauvignon (They-od-mon Chauv-ing-non): Marquis of the Westerlands of Thestitiunia. He is the equivalent of a Duke for all intents and purposes, however, due to the faerie lands on his lands; his acreage is shy of what's needed for the legal title of 'Duke'. He is a liaison for the humans and Faeries as his father was before him, and his father was, and so forth. He is married to Amaria Raulet. A talented military strategist and swordsman.

Henri Delaluna (Henry De-la-luna): An Extractor. He can read minds, control and alter thoughts, and change memories. He is from the Westerlands, Thestitiunia, and while currently an untitled Lord, once his father passes he will be a Marquis.

Lynette Edrion (Lynn-et Ed-ree-on): Mentioned. The Queen of Avondra. Is one of the people behind the recent attacks on Amaria Raulet's ancestral home.

Delphina Ginsery (Del-fein-na Gin-ser-ray): Mentioned. Deceased. Thestitiunian noblewoman from the Perivina Fluere province who is murdered during the attack on Provincia Palencia in which the Raulet Ruby is stolen.

Nicoletta Lemaire (Nicoletta Lay-may-er): Soon to be Countess Nicoletta Astasuel as she is engaged to Jaques Astasuel, a Westanni Earl. She was born in Raulle, in Perivina Fluere, Thestitiunia. She has been a lady-in-waiting and friend to Amaria Raulet since she was a child.

Livia Maiges (Liv-e-aah May-ge-ess): A minor Westanni noblewoman. Theodmon Chauvignon's old mistress.

Katerina Montersatt (Cat-err-ein-ah Mon-teer-saat): Healing mage who works for the Chauvignons at Forteresse les Blanche.

Clarissa Nalaeny (Clare-iss-aa Nale-aah-len-knee): Mentioned. The sister of the king of Rindria. Is one of the people behind the recent attacks on Amaria Raulet's ancestral home.

Aaron Raulet (Aaron Raul-lay): The Duke of the Perivina Fluere Province of Thestitiunia. Cold, ruthless, and cunning, he is efficient in getting his political goals accomplished.

Amaria Raulet (Am-mar-ree-ah Raul-lay): Also known as Marchioness Amaria Chauvignon. She is an Extractor, a powerful elemental mage, able to control the elements of water and earth ("Hydra Blessed") as well as fire and air ("Dragon Blessed"). She is the wife of Theodmon Chauvignon and mother of Lysander Chauvignon. She is Aaron and Illyana Raulet's oldest child and the twin of Haerdnor.

Catalina Raulet (Cat-ah-lein-ah Raul-lay): Mentioned. The youngest daughter of Aaron and Illyana Raulet. She survived a deathly childhood illness that left her with golden scars over her face and throat. She is training to enter a Temple of Ignoia (the healing goddess).

Haerdnor Raulet (Hair-den-noir Raul-lay): The oldest son of Aaron and Illyana Raulet. A hot headed fire mage, he is brave and arrogant. The younger twin of Amaria. In a secret relationship with Oliver Neremoux.

Illyana Raulet (Ill-ee-ann-aah Raul-lay): Mentioned. Deceased. A Duchess. Married to Aaron Raulet. Originally from Tressidil, her brother is the current Lord Prime Minister of Tressidil. Mother to Amaria, Haerdnor, and Catalina Raulet.

Durek Svilas (Dur-rek Civ-vil-az): A Morrian Duke. He married the eldest daughter of the Morrian King. Was at Amaria and Theodmon's wedding.

Lyseno Vypren (Lis-sen-no Vie-pren): Mentioned. The Duke of Darcassa, Avondra. Amaria Raulet's ex-fiancé. He is an angry, bitter man, feeling as if he were embarrassed internationally because of it.

Thestitiunia (Thes-tit-tune-ee-ah)

Thestitiunia is an empire comprised of five provinces, Perivina Fluere, the Westerlands, Lierre Fideles, Arbres Dorés, and Sauvegarde Corolline. Each province is ruled by a Duke (or in the Westerlands' case, a Marquis). These provinces are almost like "mini-kingdoms" within the empire, each province is larger than both the sovereign nations of Rindria and Tressidil. Perivina Fluere is larger than the sovereign of Morroek. Thestitiunia is the richest nation, as well as the most aggressive militarily. Magic is highly valued here.

The Westerlands

The Westerlands is the north-west province in Thestitiunia with Morroek to the north, Rindria to the west, Lierre Fideles to the east, Sauvegarde Corolline to the south, and in the eastern southernmost part of the Westerlands there is shared border with Arbres Dorés. Many forests, farms, and mines, and weapons industry. The ruling family is the Chauvignon. The Westerlands ruling family is a Marquis as due to the faerielands they are just shy of the acreage needed for Thestitiunian Dukehood.

The entrance to the faeries' lands is located here, with the ruling family acting as liaisons between humans and faeries. A wild place, it is blessed with the highest percentage of mages per capita in the empire, as well as the rest of the world. However, wild and magical animals roam free and it can be a dangerous place if you are not careful. The people are called Westannis and/or Thestitiunians, depending on the regional or imperial context. Westannis can be stern and militaristic, however, they tend to be community-oriented. The Westerands host the strongest standing Army in the empire.

Adanes (Aah-dann-nees): A town to the south of the Faerielands.

Auberville (Aub-ber-ville): A westernmost city in the Westerlands. Borders the mountains that separates the Westerlands from the Nagalia Aride desert.

Chauvi (Chauv-vee): The capital city of the Westerlands and the seat of power for the Chauvignons.

Dovesport (Dovesport): A small city to the east of Lake Holimeda. Borders the Faerielands.

The faerie lands: The mysterious forest in which the fae live.

Forteresse les Blanche (Fort-eer-esse les Blan-ch-ay): The castle of the Chauvignons. It is carved from Mount Mortensia. It is incredibly fortified with a pulley system designed to bring in supplies.

Lake Holimeda (Lake Hal-ee-me-dah): The large body of water by Chauvi, Dovesport, and the Faerielands.

Maulleries (Maul-lur-ees): A fortress town near Perives Pass and the Westanni-Riam border.

Monsa (Mon-sah): A small lakeside town that's south of the Faerielands.

Mortensia Labyrinths (Moort-tiin-cee-aah Laa-bre-inths): The Chauvignon maintained dungeons and prisons. Tends to be harsh and dark—the only light comes from torches, there are no windows and there is only one entrance and exit into the prison.

Mount Mortensia (Mount Moort-tiin-cee-aah): The Mountain on which Forteresse les Blanche is carved from. It also hosts the Mortensia Labyrinths carved deep on the inside of the mountain.

Perpives Pass (Per-pii-vees Pass): A natural gap in the mountains between Rindria and the Westerlands. Heavily armored and fortified on both sides of the border due to the Riam-Thestitiunian distrust of each other.

Valemont Tunnels (Valemont Tunnels): The maintained entrance between the Westerlands and Morroek. The mountains were carved to allow this wide tunnel between the nations for travel and trade. It it heavily fortified on both sides of the border, due to Morrian-Thestitiunian distrust of each other.

Valeville (Vale-ville): A fortress town near Valemont and the Westanni-Morrian border.

Victorie ("Victory"): A Westanni town to the south, some of the city crosses into the Arbres Dorés province and is a few miles outside of the Lierre Fideles province to the east and the Sauvegarde Coroline province to the south.

Enjoy a sneak peak of the next book in the Curoria Chronicles, *The Topaz Crown:*

Theodmon's forehead was clammy, however his hands didn't shake as he carried his sword and shield. Outside the battlements of Aionstown, his small force of rebellious nobles, mages, and their men remained waiting for dusk to settle.

When dusk settled, they would rush through the sewers, going as rats to the Imperial Palace as Aion continued to execute rebellious nobles and mages he had captured. As far as Theodmon could tell, Aion must have had around six-hundred captured.

Aion had been publicly executing these people—around ten to fifteen every night. Perhaps, according to all the sources Theodmon had, there were five hundred or so still living. Amaria was included in those captured souls. As if panic was trapped in a jar, Theodmon felt it stirring inside of him. How could he be sure she wasn't dead? Aion would likely want to kill her first—she was prolific, an instigator of the fall of his rule.

Theodmon hoped that she was alive. However, even if she wasn't, he'd save all those countrymen from their capture, kill the emperor and rid this country of the rot that plagued it. Theodmon would install himself as the new governor and bring justice for the deaths of those brave enough to rebel.

He would rule for both him and Amaria so as to honor her memory.

He turned to face his troops, the sewage on the sand sloshing around his feet. "There's five hundred of our countrymen captured there! If we don't defeat Aion tonight, they're as good as dead."

And so are we.

"Five hundred lives are at stake, and there's just one life to take to save them!" Haerdnor screamed, his hands lighting on fire. The only thing brighter than his hands were the maniacal look in his eyes. Theodmon believed that all Raulets were touched with greatness but they were equally touched with madness—and Haerdnor's had broken through with the capture of his father and twin. "Kill Aion Marion, and this hell will end."

"We have no backup. We will be surrounded. We will likely suffer heavy losses," Theodmon told them gravely. "But we have five hundred reasons to fight. Those captured are our spouses, our parents, our children, and our siblings. We have every reason to try, and no reason to accept failure."

"We can avoid blood–" Faelyn began to say.

"No," the other healer, Katerina snarled. "Bloodshed is unavoidable."

"You're a healer–"

"And the removal of a tumor is an innately violent process," Katerina snapped. "A bloodless peace is a fragile one that will break as it's taken for granted."